A Man Lost

Helen Bland

Grosvenor House
Publishing Limited

This book is published by
Grosvenor House Publishing Ltd
Link House
140 The Broadway, Tolworth, Surrey, KT6 7HT.
www.grosvenorhousepublishing.co.uk

Disclaimer:-

The characters in this novel are entirely fictitious and bear no
reference or relation to any person either living or deceased.

A CIP record for this book
is available from the British Library

ISBN 978-1-80381-339-4

For my sister Kay and brother Peter

Book one in The Roxberg Trilogy

The Other Sister

Art gallery curator Giselle Villande and her husband, an antique dealer from Menton in the south of France, find themselves drawn into an insidious web of poisoning and murder motivated by financial greed and sexual jealousy

Nebulous tendrils of evil draw them still further to Paris and Honfleur then finally to Giselle's isolated family home, Roxberg Gate, on the wild and beautiful Northumbrian coast.

In this sexually-charged labyrinthine conspiracy a plot is conceived to undermine and ultimately destroy Giselle's family.

Book two in The Roxberg Trilogy

The Spanish Widow

After the birth of her second daughter, Inez Roxberg a wealthy spirited artist from Madrid, distanced herself from her unfaithful husband, his mistress, and their love child to pursue an uninhibited bohemian life in France. Many years later, standing at his graveside, she vowed never again to relinquish her wealth and power to anyone.

Her late husband's final gift of a long-case clock becomes an ill-fated harbinger of sinister deceptions calculated to steal her wealth and erode her sanity. When two men enter her life, one a bold adventurer, the other a tantalising libertine each with their own hidden agenda, who will she choose, who dare she trust with her life?

Haunted to the point of obsession by the tragic death of her eldest daughter, Honoré, Inez embarks on a quest to discover the truth and serve justice on her killer. Oblivious to the destructive forces surrounding her, Inez unknowingly descends into a criminal underworld of art forgery, a forced marriage and death.

Prologue

In this tense concluding novel in 'The Roxberg Trilogy', we find reckless art dealer and restaurant owner Gaston Villande in more trouble than he can handle since abandoning his playboy bachelor life to marry Giselle Roxberg, the daughter of wealthy English landowner Henry Roxberg and his estranged wife Inez. The couple's volatile ten-year marriage begins to unravel when sordid crimes from her family's past surface, threatening to erode not only their marriage but ultimately their lives. A series of family deaths, including that of an unscrupulous fortune hunter, results in Gaston himself becoming the hunted. As his life spirals out of control, his very existence becomes a battle for survival.

Cast of Characters

Gaston Villande – Husband of Giselle
A beguiling French art and antique dealer in his late thirties, a dark-haired, wilful hedonist with humorous soft brown eyes, both he and his wife are co-owners of Café Villande.

Giselle Villande – Wife of Gaston – Daughter of Inez
A spirited art historian and curator of exhibitions, in her early twenties, tall and lithe, with her mother's titian hair, green eyes, and hot temper.

Iona Kerr – Chef/Manager at Café Villande
This midlife, well travelled Northumbrian chef moved from Roxberg Gate to Menton at Gaston's request. Her flaxen hair and sparkling blue eyes prove an effective antidote to her severe forthright nature.

Flora Innes – Management trainee at Café Villande
A coltish, tender-hearted young woman with billowing tawny curls and magnetic hazel eyes. An orphan who regards Gaston as something more than a father figure.

Inez Faconi – Widow of Henry Roxberg and Guido Faconi – Mother of Giselle
This tall, radiant, 50-something artist has overcome many of life's personal challenges; her strength is her resilient zest for life.

Venerio Faconi – Cousin by marriage to Inez Faconi
A stocky, swarthy complexioned, midlife bachelor devoid of interpersonal skills. He favours physical force over diplomacy, which invariably results in the death or destruction of his opponents.

Alex Forbes – Manager at *La Maison des Artistes*
An exuberant ex-Army adventurer, now in his mid-50s, with smoky blue eyes and fair hair, is a stalwart protector of Inez.

Vivienne Villande – Mama of Gaston – Wife of Maurice
A petite, fiercely academic professor of Greek philosophy, now in her mid-70s, she has no need of friends nor family; her studies are her life.

Maurice Villande – Papa of Gaston
This 70-something, ebullient owner of an antiquarian bookshop has earned a well-deserved reputation for attracting numerous friends of both sexes since retiring to Antibes.

Aria – Au-pair to baby Luc.
A self-possessed, 30-something female, of Moroccan decent, with unfathomable dark eyes and long raven hair.

Chapter One
Menton, France, 2017

A strengthening February sun warmed my face, as I stood on the doorstep calling last minute instructions to Flora.

'Bon voyage, Gaston,.' she called back, smiling as she waved from an upstairs window.

'Back in two days. Look after Giselle… and keep your dog out of my kitchen.'

Leaving the café, I sauntered to the car, savouring the heady scent of winter jasmine filling the crisp morning air heralding the promise of an early spring.

The day had dawned bright and clear, and it felt so good; in fact, exhilaratingly fantastic. I had triumphed. Guido Faconi, the enemy of my entire family was dead. Time now to return to some semblance of normality.

Next month, Giselle and I would become first-time parents. Our son's arrival would open a new chapter in our marriage, bringing a much-needed focus to our failing relationship. Since becoming pregnant, Giselle's violent outbursts have become a daily occurrence. She has no wish to become a mother; her studied indifference to any mention of 'the mistake' is ignored.

'Flora will organise the nursery and care for the child, I have no maternal instincts to ignite,' she would say defiantly. When she speaks to me, her voice holds traces of bitterness and her resentful looks chill my heart. She blames me for 'the mistake', her repeated mantra of 'I'm not ready' ringing in my ears with the regularity of a church bell.

My own well of patience has since dried to a trickle, and our staff despair of ever returning to the riotous café lifestyle we had known and loved. In recent months, the burden of restraining Giselle's verbal sniping has fallen, as always, on young Flora's shoulders. Her calming presence and reassuring manner appear to be the only antidote to Giselle's volatile outbursts. And as her self-obsession grows, she fails to notice Flora is no longer a child. The past year has seen her blossom into an unnervingly beautiful young woman – not quite young enough to be considered a daughter, but certainly old enough to become a lover.

Scudding rain clouds slipped across the sun, sending a shiver of apprehension up my spine. I glanced around, wary of strangers, my fear heightened by thoughts of encountering Venerio, cousin of Guido Faconi, the man I had deliberately pushed to his death over the harbour wall at Villefranche.

If Venerio suspected me of his cousin's murder, he would come looking for me.

My life, and that of my entire family, will remain under threat until I find a way of silencing him. Venerio is a lawless thug, who would maim or murder to avenge his deceitful cousin or to satisfy his own greed and warped sense of honour.

I reached to rub my left shoulder. It was still painful from the stab wound inflicted by Guido's brother Allesio, now serving a lengthy prison sentence for conspiring in the murder of Giselle's long departed sister, Honore.

I couldn't help but think of how different my life would have been if I had never met Giselle Roxberg and her sister Honore on that summer day at my café in Menton.

I didn't regret pushing a chancer like Guido Faconi to his death; he had it coming for infiltrating my family with the sole intention of robbing us of our wealth. And I was determined that if Venerio came within a mile of any one of us, he would suffer a similar fate.

My urgent need to escape life's pressures had reached a tipping point. I wanted to get drunk and make endless passionate love to Flora. Images of her inviting smile and soft teasing voice circulated in my mind, leaving me madly frustrated and extremely horny. If asked, my papa would advise me to seek sexual solace in a Parisian pleasure house, as he had done for most of his married life – much to the relief of Mama! Not for me, though. Only pure pulsating love will satisfy my romantic lusts.

Casting carnal thoughts aside, I turned my attention to the serious business of constructing a plausible confession and one that Giselle would accept. But how does one tell a wife she has married a murderer? And how do I find a safe avenue of escape when she explodes in temper and blames me for everything. Surely Giselle will accept the motivation that drove me to commit this crime of expediency; surely *she* will not condemn me for an act calculated to save our whole family from ruinous destruction. But then, how can I tell her – the wife from whom I hide nothing of myself – or indeed tell anyone of that fateful day when thoughts of murder entered my mind.

Leaning back against the headrest, I closed my eyes, recalling the images of Guido's terror-stricken face as he fought against the swirling, white-tipped waves.

When he stood, proud and arrogant, my enemy, the enemy of my family, oblivious to anything other than his own selfish desires, a raging well of anger had risen inside me. And it had been *so* easy. He had made it easy, standing above those steep, slippery steps leading down from the harbour to the icy waters below.

Slumped in my car seat, a black fedora pulled low over my eyes, I had watched and waited as a dense, swirling sea mist seeped stealthily into the late afternoon twilight, enabling me to approach him from behind when he came out of the house. Pacing the harbour, oblivious to the howling wind and poor visibility, he continued shouting into his mobile phone, while thrusting an angry fist into the air. He neither saw nor heard my footsteps approaching. One tremendous push and it was all over.

I watched with callous disregard as he hit the electric cable floating just inches above the dark foaming water, his body writhing and scorching as he flayed, his screams tempered by a suffocating veil of thick grey mist rolling in from the sea.

'Curse you!' he screamed, as powerful currents tossed his vibrating body like flotsam against the harbour wall, and I felt nothing. Nothing except relief at seeing my enemy contort himself to hell.

Turning away, I wondered if we would ever be free of him or his tainted associations with Giselle's parents.

In recent months, our family had endured enough tragedy to fill two lifetimes. Faconi had forced his way into our family, issuing threats and using emotional blackmail in order to steal our family's considerable wealth – Giselle's inheritance; our son's inheritance. What right had he to steal what should in time become

CHAPTER ONE

ours by right, blighting our future, leaving us with the devastating consequences of his greed? Well, it ended at my hand, without sorrow or regret.

Fastening the seatbelt, I searched the inside pocket of my overcoat and took out my papa's old Beretta. The sensuous feeling of cold metal on my skin gave me a powerful surge of reassurance. After loading the weapon, I quickly returned it to its hiding place inside my coat.

Ok, Venerio, I'm ready. You're next.

Leaning forward to press the call button marked Papa, I waited, and he answered after three rings, his bellicose voice rising to full volume.

'Bonjour, bonjour, Gaston my son,' Maurice bellowed down the line. 'So you're still alive after dealing with those Faconi brothers. Pay us a visit, we want to hear your news.' He guffawed loudly.

He couldn't fool me, though. I could hear his concern, all nicely hidden beneath a chorus of mirth.

'Actually, I am on my way to you now, if it's convenient, but without Giselle. I have an appointment to value a picture tomorrow afternoon in Antibes and thought to pay you and Mama a visit. How did the house move go? Are you missing Paris yet?'

After a long pause and a sharp intake of breath, he said, 'Not missing Paris one bit. No more city life for me; the coast is more to my liking. The natives are friendly, in fact very friendly, and the food is exquisite. Not sure your mama would agree, though.' He chuckled. 'Now, Gaston, your appointment – not an assignation with a pretty woman, I hope.'

'Definitely not. One woman is quite enough, especially one with Giselle's uncertain temperament.

5

My nerves just wouldn't hold up,' I answered untruthfully, as an image of Flora's face floated into my mind.

'You'll find me in the square with a book in one hand and a glass of rouge in the other. Oh, and for once drive carefully. See you shortly,' he bellowed with laughter before switching the phone off.

I pressed the engine start button while appraising my reflection in the rear-view mirror. Deep, dark circles rimmed my eyes; my face, sallow and sagging from exhaustion, looked old and lifeless.

Giselle's family have made a murderer of me.

Just then, Alex Forbes rang. *What now?* I thought warily. *Not more family dramas.*

'Bonjour, Alex, is this business or pleasure?' I asked impatiently, while closing the car window to exclude the noise of oncoming traffic.

'Both. Now, Gaston, you old trickster, we need to talk. Where are you? I have some interesting news,' said Alex teasingly.

'On my way to Antibes, if it's any business of yours,' I replied testily.

'Ok, ok, just making conversation, no need to bite. So, what's eating you? Anyone would think someone died.'

'Oh, very amusing.' A pulse quickened in my neck. *Is this guy trying to spook me?* 'If you must know, I am on my way to mix business with a parental visit.'

'Ok, fine, it can wait until we meet,' Alex replied lightly, a note of humour in his voice.

'Why the subterfuge? Why not tell me now?' I replied tersely.

'I would rather wait until we meet. I want to see your expression.'

'Oh right, so you're going to arrest me.'

'You forget I resigned, so no, I won't be doing any arresting. Might snitch on you, though, if you don't behave yourself.'

'Go hang yourself, Alex,' I said irritably and switched off.

A few moments later, the phone rang again.

'Ok crazy guy, you listen to me,' said Alex angrily. 'Lucky for you the cops have decided Guido had a heart attack. By their reckoning, it's the most plausible explanation for his so-called accident. Only you and I know differently, because I videoed the whole thing.'

A sudden surge of anger sent blood pounding through my ears, bringing a flush to my face and a dangerous edge to my voice. This so-called ex-cop was exceeding his remit.

'So what do you intend to do, turn me in and risk alienating Inez? No, you need the job... and incidentally, keep your hands off my mother-in-law and my son's inheritance. Then forget what you think you saw, unless you want to join Faconi in hell.'

'Too late where Inez and I are concerned; that ship sailed some time ago. We are together – a fact you need to accept, for everyone's sake. So ok, Gaston, here's the deal. For the moment, I will park what I know I saw, out of respect for Inez, your wife, and her unborn son. But don't get any ideas about my silence being in anyway permanent. You need to wise up, man. You need to get real and appreciate what you have.'

'Yeah, and when I need advice from you, you'll be the first to know. Until then, keep your mouth shut and stay out of my business.'

'From now on, your business *is* my business,' said Alex forcibly, his voice laden with threat. 'Enjoy your parental visit, as it may be some time before you see them again.'

Alex switched off, leaving me open-mouthed and seething with resentment. Damn him to hell! He could ruin everything just as Guido had intended, had he been allowed to live. And now, if Alex and Inez married, nothing changed – Giselle's inheritance could be lost, only this time to a guy with incontrovertible evidence of my murderous act of revenge.

Depressing my foot on the accelerator, I drove on at speed, my mind everywhere but on my own safety. After a few tortuous miles, I pulled into a roadside café in need of a strong drink. Once inside, I thought better of it and ordered a non-alcoholic beer, from a sinuous looking waitress wearing a clean, but clearly well-worn apron and a welcoming expression.

The beer tasted vile, so I drank it down, then ordered a glass of crisp white wine to cleanse my offended palate. The waitress drew my attention to various plates of un-covered cold buffet, surrounded by crumbs and other food debris, loitering on the countertop near the coffee machine.

'You are not hungry, *monsieur*?' she enquired haughtily, raising her black-pencilled brows. 'Perhaps your appetites are of a more personal nature – a neck massage perhaps, to relieve your stress. You are stressed, that much is obvious.' She gave me a knowing wink as she produced two menus: the first, neatly hand- written in bold black lettering on red paper, with time-limited descriptions of the services available, including prices for extras; the second listed the questionable delights found mouldering on the countertop, all of which looked unhygienic and well past their sell-by date.

Tactfully declining her offer of both, I paid the bill and bolted for the door.

Back on the road, feeling relieved to have escaped the unwanted attentions of the grubby waitress, my thoughts turned to Inez and her intentions regarding that joker Alex Forbes. I wanted to know how far their relationship had progressed, so perhaps a little detour on the way home would be a good idea. However, seeing her alone without Alex's influence and potential interference might prove difficult, as he constantly hovered in the background whenever Giselle or I called.

Yes, a pleasant drive to Villefranche will improve my mood, I thought glibly. Inez was a generous, fair-minded woman, who would improve the mood of any man, including a self-righteous prig like Alex Forbes.

My mood lightened a little as I sped along the coast road in the direction of Antibes. I hoped a few days free of Giselle's temper and, if my nerve held, a soul-bearing conversation with Papa, would help to sort my head out.

Driving on at a steady pace with my stomach churning, irrational fears began to take shape in my mind, magnifying tenfold as my journey's end drew closer.

I had committed an unforgivable crime and one that would incur a long prison sentence if I were caught. My parents – or Papa in particular – were adept at reading my behaviour. Would he notice the edge in my voice, or the nervous twitch in my cheek? I had not seen either of my parents for almost a year; a year in which my family had been torn apart. It was time for me to move on, to distance myself from the past and recapture my old life, or re-invent the current one.

Arriving in Antibes, I drove directly to the main car park. The sun was relentlessly hot for early spring and the main streets were crowded with tourists looking for a shaded spot to escape the heat. Any one of these people could be Venerio, as I had little or no recollection of him, although Inez would have no difficulty in describing 'the odious cousin', as she often referred to him.

I felt strung out and in need of a cognac in order to face Mama. No doubt she would greet me with her usual coolness, which is not unreasonable given the past difficulties in our relationship. We had nothing in common and no shared interests; any feelings between us are borne out of duty rather than affection.

Papa's nature, in contrast, is much like my own. Our easy humour and keen sense of the ridiculous had latterly saved many an awkward family argument from becoming a permanent estrangement. But now even my perennial optimism was in short supply.

I sauntered leisurely into the labyrinth of narrow back streets, with a bright yellow sun in my eyes, and the intoxicating scent of tree sap and pink blossom mingling together from newly formed spring buds merging into salt-filled air.

I wondered which of my parents had chosen this enchanting place to spend their retirement, particularly as their personal tastes differed to extremes.

Sitting at a street bar, sipping a double cognac, my thoughts receded into a soft focus, imagining my perfect life. All around me were convivial scenes of Francophile residents mingling with tourists, all jostling for restaurant seats, or calling out to friends as they wandered home after an expensive afternoon shopping, or visiting the bustling food market in search of fresh produce and easy entertainment. How I envied their untroubled lives, their relaxed nonchalance, lingering conversations, and casual smiles. Life was precious, and I wanted my life to be as good as it could get. And no-one, especially a chancer like Alex Forbes, was going to prevent me from having it all.

Papa and I had arranged to meet in the main square. Apparently, his homing pigeon instinct had not as yet bedded in, which frequently resulted in him losing his bearings when attempting to find the home he shared, albeit intermittently, with Mama.

'Where the hell is this square?' I said under my breath, after taking yet another wrong turn. Fishing the phone from my pocket, I offered up a silent prayer that Papa would answer my call. He answered on the second ring.

'Right now, I'll keep talking until you find me,' he said enthusiastically.

Then, annoyingly, he began recounting various snippets of news from his daily life. I asked him to stop and to save his news until dinner, when we would all be gathered together with a glass of something inside us. It would take the edge off Mama's spear-head comments. But no, he continued to regale me with such urgency that I was quite taken aback by his vehemence.

'Of course, my days are now divided between the square and my bookshop. Your mama is disinterested in anything that isn't either ancient or Greek; I can manage one but not the other.' He let out a whoop of laughter.

Papa in haphazard fashion had not forwarded me their new address when they had moved two weeks previously, and he had already lost several scraps of paper on which the address and directions were written.

'Don't worry, I know where my bookshop is, it's the house I have trouble finding. These streets all look alike.' Papa's chuckle rang in my ear. 'Unsurprisingly, your mama has declined to join us; she has a deadline to meet and will see us at home later on.' He sighed wearily, then dropped the phone and began swearing softly.

Eventually I found him sitting in the square, his bleary eyes squinting through half-rimmed spectacles, his nose planted between the pages of a racy book, and a half-finished glass of wine on the table in front of him. His look of sublime contentment sent waves of guilt washing over me.

Then he saw me, and my heart lurched at the sight of him. I realised at that very moment how much I had missed him, his unfailing good humour, and the protective sense of strength he exuded.

'Ah, Gaston, my son. Come, come.' He came forward and gave me a gut-wrenching hug. The familiar smell of old leather and pipe tobacco emanated from his clothing, aromas so blindingly reminiscent of my childhood – a time when the adult world was a foreign place and blissfully unknown to me.

'Pardon, Papa, where is the toilet? My bowels are calling.'

Papa indicated to the café opposite. 'Not my influence, I hope,' he called after me as I bolted through the nearest café entrance door. He was still half doubled with laughter as I emerged, his shoulders shaking uncontrollably at my embarrassment.

'Fine for you retired oldies, sitting around with no knowledge of where you are or what year we're in,' I teased.

'Ah, you just wait, young man. Retirement is marvellous, although your mama reckons I have been retired since birth.' He grimaced over his raised glass.

After a few sips of wine, I felt sufficiently recovered enough to contemplate a binding brunch of olive bread toasted and smothered in melted brie and overripe tomatoes.

My unscheduled comfort break had allowed Papa the opportunity of engaging a well-preserved female, of an undefinable age, in deep conversation. He introduced her as an avid bibliophile friend. She gave me a coy look, leaned forward, and placed her hand on my sleeve.

'Your papa and I read Dumas and Voltaire together in his bookshop some afternoons. We have recently become firm friends,' she purred in my ear. The old rascal; didn't take him long to assuage his loneliness with an attractive woman.

It was easy to understand why Papa preferred this woman's lively conversation to Mama's curt responses, as they were polar opposites.

We sat for a while discussing art and literature. As the day shortened, the salty air became chilled and damp, and both locals and tourists began to filter away. I suggested we continue indoors which, to my relief, prompted Papa's friend to leave. After bidding her a warm *adieu*, we ordered dark chocolate and cardamom tarts, accompanied by a bottle of seriously extravagant cognac, then settled comfortably in a discreet corner to talk.

l offered Papa a severely edited version of the events which had occurred in my life over the past six months, and his facial expressions alternated between incredulous surprise and outraged fury.

'Ah yes, Faconi ' he said thoughtfully, stroking his chin. 'Now there's a name from the past. A rather surly looking young man with the same name turned up unexpectedly at the apartment prior to our leaving Paris. I was out, lunching with friends at the time. But your mama remarked how ill at ease he seemed. She described him as being strangely familiar, said she'd heard of the name but not the man. I arrived home to find her looking shocked and quite unnerved; she said she was glad to be rid of him. He claimed to be a friend of yours, said he'd lost your phone number and needed to get in touch, so she gave him your home number and our new address, in case we needed to pass you a message. In fact, he did leave a message for you. Ask her about it later.'

A quiver of apprehension ran up my spine as I speculated as to which member of the Faconi family had taken the trouble to seek out my parents. Allesio, most likely, as he was known to have stayed in Paris around that time, and if *he* knew of my parents' whereabouts, then Venerio would know, too.

'Bastards all of them,' I muttered through clenched teeth.

'What's that? If you're in trouble, better say now before we meet Mama,' said Papa, looking ruffled.

'It's not important. Just family disputes, all resolved now,' I replied, more in hope than certainty.

'Mama has insisted on cooking tonight.' Papa pulled a dubious face.

'I'm afraid my drains won't stand the onslaught of Mama's weird concoctions. Let's persuade her to eat out.'

'Good idea, safety in numbers and all that,' he said wryly.

My mama did not have the slightest interest in cooking; she considered it a waste of her valuable time, as their house – geographically speaking – was surrounded by a cornucopia of excellent restaurants. Having just recovered from one bout of the runs, I resigned myself to being found in a similar position very soon if Mama was allowed a free rein in the kitchen.

'If Mama insists on inflicting her less than *haute cuisine* on us tonight, I will make some excuse then resurrect my explosive gut.'

'Good idea. Might follow your lead,' said Papa with a conspiratorial grin. 'Your mama has been attempting to undermine my constitution with her culinary disasters for most of our interminably lengthy marriage. More so since she discovered my predilection for female friends. I told her I have a business to develop. What is a bookshop without customers?' He raised a bushy eyebrow and winked.

'So, tell me, did she bring her vulgar ornaments? Or did you pay the removal men to accidentally throw them down the stairs?'

'Wouldn't have dared; worth more than my life. She hasn't unpacked yet. I hoped you might take them back to Menton and flog them to the tourists,' said Papa with a cheeky grin.

'No thanks. I have a reputable antique emporium, not a junk shop!'

Until recently, my parents had resided for some 30 years in a large apartment in central Paris, in which time Mama had accumulated vast amounts of tasteless bric-a-brac, most of which she has refused to give up. This motley collection was now stored in expensive wooden crates, costing considerably more than their contents.

'Well, if you're still living out of crates, we will definitely be dining out,' I said firmly.

'We live like lodgers about to depart,' joked Papa affably. 'Right, let me show you my little gem of a bookshop.' He rattled a bunch of keys as he struggled to his feet.

Admittedly, the quaint exterior of the tiny shop looked appealing enough and, apart from peeling paint on the windows and front door, which hung at a slight angle, even I could see its potential, being situated on a busy thoroughfare just off the main square. A pungent smell of drains assailed us as we entered the building, and decaying wallpaper hung down the walls from large patches of damp black mildew. The scuffle of mice could be heard as we climbed the narrow staircase – a paradise for worms and rodents, and an obstacle course for less than agile humans like Papa.

'A bookshop without shelves or indeed books? Interesting. Have you signed the lease?'

'No lease,' answered Papa defensively.

'Don't tell me you actually bought this place,' I retorted, looking around in disbelief.

'My sanctuary,' he beamed. 'Away from your mama's orb of control, there is a tiny apartment on the top floor where my few indulgences cannot be detected, if you take my meaning.' He winked furiously as I burst out laughing.

'Yes, Papa, you mean illicit food and drink, as anything of a carnal nature would be quite beyond your capabilities,' I replied cheekily, eyeing his corpulent waistline straining against worn red braces.

'Ah, Gaston my son, you have lost your imagination. There are pleasures to be found around every street corner,' he said, tapping his nose and smiling.

'Ok, let's take a look at your lair,' I said, giving him a doubtful look.

The old man wasn't exaggerating. After passing two floors of wholesale dereliction, to my amazement the top floor apartment had been lovingly converted into a cosy bachelor space. A cramped single bedroom led to a tiny balcony with a panoramic view of the harbour and beyond to the fort.

'Has Mama seen this place?'

Papa winced and shook his head. 'Er, partly. She opened the front door, took one step inside, then turned on her heel. She said she might consider returning when the place was fit for human habitation. I tried to explain, but she wouldn't listen, but then she never does. Didn't speak to me for a week. Eventually she found her voice and accused me of wasting her retirement fund.'

That's all I need, marital unrest among the elderly, I thought wearily.

'She has a point, though, the place looks unsafe to me. Hope you didn't pay a high price for it.'

'Bargain, my boy, bargain,' replied Papa jovially. 'Ah well, Gaston, you can talk her round. Use your famous charm; never fails.'

'I might have known you had an ulterior motive. Well, let me tell you, Mama never listens to me either. Now let's go and find her.'

Papa thrust his hand into his trouser pocket and fished out a crump_ed street plan of the town; his house was clearly marked by a red cross. He studied the paper momentarily then thrust it into my hand.

'You find it.'

'Ok, so you're telling me that after two weeks you still have trouble locating your own home?'

Papa snorted with laughter. 'Hardly ever visit; don't see the point. Your mama spends most days in her study, and my needs are never considered. Throughout our marriage, she has never been what I would term a wifely wife. I'm no longer entirely sure why we married. Of course, in retrospect I should have married a woman with fire in her belly; a woman like that mama-in-law of yours, Inez, could excite any man.' He looked away, disappointment clouding his florid features. 'Enough of me. As you say, let's go and find the old dragon.'

A reflective silence and a sense of mutual discontent hung over us as we walked along the pretty backstreets furthest from the sea.

We found Mama in her study, a converted attic on the top floor of their spacious town house. She turned and nodded in acknowledgement, then turned back, engrossing herself in a large, decrepit-looking book. Two laptop screens were switched on: one displaying statues of ancient Greeks; the other an illegible script – illegible to me, that is. Her look of myopic preoccupation had not changed over the years. Bird-like in stature, she appeared to me quite frail; more so than the picture of her lodged in my memory.

She wore a black trouser suit, which hung in folds around her slight frame. As I greeted her and walked towards her desk, she gave me a brief appraising glance then returned to her work.

'Bonjour, Gaston,' she remarked absentmindedly, without raising her head.

My hackles rose a couple of degrees. 'Bonjour, Mama.' I waited while she continued to survey the screens, cross-referencing them with the decrepit book lying open on the desk.

'Is that all you can manage after a year's absence, Mama? You take economy of speech to another level.' My sharp retort was ignored.

'We can talk over dinner… assuming you are staying,' she said, her attention never wavering from the screen. 'Ask your papa to book a restaurant, would you? I simply haven't time for cooking.'

'Ask him yourself, for heaven's sake. He is standing here. What is wrong with you?'

'Ask your papa. His implausible lies will no doubt appeal to the less palatable side of your nature. Now, please excuse me, Gaston, my publishing deadline is fast approaching. We can talk later,' she replied dismissively.

'Right… fine… Only you won't be seeing *me* later. Papa and I will dine out together.'

'As you wish,' she said, without a flicker of emotion.

I turned to Papa as we slammed the front door behind us.

'What the hell is the matter with her?' I yelled in exasperation.

Papa shrugged. 'You see, I told you your mama has lost all sociability. What little she had has shrivelled to the size of a walnut; a very hard walnut. She resents my friends, both male and female, and now seemingly she resents even you.' He shook his head, a look of resignation on his face.

'Then why do you stay with her?' I asked irritably.

Papa paused momentarily. 'I do what most French husbands do in such circumstances, and find solace in other women. Over the years my friends have supported me and have infused my life with varying degrees of the happiness so lacking in a marriage dulled by layers of sour words, calculated to prick any balloon of joy to be found in life. And now, life is what I intend to have in spades.' He punched the air and walked on, humming under his breath.

After a few minutes, he turned to me. 'Of course, your mama suspects my occasional lapses and has become habitually resentful of any pleasure garnered through friends. The unpalatable truth is that she never loved me; I am a disappointment to her.' He threw up his hands in a gesture of hopelessness.

My anger grew as we retraced our steps to the square, in search of a restaurant with tables to spare. Feelings of guilt flooded over me at my neglect and infrequent visits since marrying Giselle.

'I can find no warmth in Mama, and God knows I have looked. The whole of my lonely, miserable childhood was spent yearning for any gesture, any look of affection from her.'

'My fault. I should have left her and found you a true mama. Too late now, she will have to suffice. Together we will make her suffice,' he added.

Finding an unoccupied table with a narrow view of the harbour, we decided to eat outdoors, underneath a large, heated canopy. The sharp evening air filled our nostrils with the mouth-watering smell of roasting meat – a speciality of this particular restaurant, according to Papa – in contrast to the mainly seafood establishments around the square. We ordered cocktails, then settled down to read our menus.

As we sipped, my mood softened. Time and the forthcoming birth of my son would, undoubtedly, banish any negative thoughts gathering like storm clouds overhead.

Minutes later, Mama rang to say she would be joining us after all. She apologised for her offhand welcome and asked which restaurant we had chosen. Welcoming an opportunity to speak with her alone, I suggested we meet outside her front door while Papa finished his drink – time to hear her version of what Papa had, or had not done to incur her total indifference to him.

Mama appeared after a few minutes, wearing a long black coat thrown over her trouser suit, making her look crow-like, severe, and frighteningly unapproachable.

'Well, Mama, we are honoured. I can't remember the last time we all dined out together.'

'No sarcasm, please, Gaston,' she murmured, sailing past me.

Just as I had been looking forward to a boys' night out and a confessional with Papa, the angel of doom had decided to spoil our evening. As we walked, she put her arm through mine, which could only mean one thing: a lecture on neglectful behaviour!

'Gaston, if you don't mind my saying, you look completely wrecked. I spoke with Giselle this morning just after you left. The dear girl poured her heart out, so I know everything, and considerably more than you.' She stopped and stared me out.

'I must insist you stop meddling in the past. No good can come of it and, from what I hear, you have been interfering in dangerous matters that are none of your business,' she retorted imperiously.

'Mama, this is unfair. You are condemning me without a hearing.'

I came to a halt and insisted she hear me out, so we sat outside a tiny bar selling cocktails and tapas. I ordered two large glasses of Chablis, rang Papa to advise him of our short delay, then launched into my version of life with my infamous in-laws.

'Mama, since marrying Giselle, I have fallen victim to the intrigues and dramas consuming her family's lives. You have no idea how stressful just being part of her life can be. Ok, she will have offered you her forthright opinions. However, you must listen to me. I mean, really listen.'

'Yes, Gaston, no doubt, but first you must listen to me. It may surprise you to hear that many years ago, your papa had tenuous business connections to the Faconis, connections that fortunately for us have now ended. If you have already discussed this with him, be in no doubt that Papa will have lied to you about ever knowing them, or denied having any knowledge of their criminal activities. After speaking with Giselle this morning, it would appear they have not forgotten us, which explains Allesio's visit to our home in Paris.

'I seem to remember your papa had a small share in a diamond mine somewhere out in Africa. About ten years ago, the family offered a fair price for his share. Refusing to comply with their demands could have meant trouble, so he sold out.

At the time, I was completely absorbed in my own career and totally disinterested in his. The exact nature of their business together still eludes me, however I clearly remembered their name and the anguished tones of his parents on hearing the mere mention of it. Many years ago, we heard – through a third party – news of a female child having been born into the Faconi family. Unconfirmed rumours abounded that Guido was the father.'

'Mama, let me stop you there. You're telling me Guido has a daughter – an heir to his estate, stepsister to Giselle, and potential claim on my son's future inheritance?'

'Yes, we thought you all knew. Now, Gaston, do keep up. Apparently her mother, a deeply religious type, teaches English out in some exotic country. We heard she disappeared with the child when marriage was denied her. It's complicated, so I won't bore you with more details.'

'You're not boring me, Mama. On the contrary, for once you have my full attention.'

'Gaston, the Faconis are a dangerous family. They inhabit an underworld beyond your comprehension, so you would be well advised to avoid any contact with them. Suffice to say, stay out of their way and, more importantly, out of their business.'

'Mama, tell me why Allesio visited you in Paris and what message he left for me.' She sighed and looked away again, searching for words to explain why she had not shared this vital piece of information earlier.

'Gaston, I have known of Allesio and his brother Guido's existence since they were children. Contact between our two families ended years ago – that is, until recently. I was shocked beyond words to hear of Inez's encounter with Guido. Giselle tells me he died quite suddenly. How fortunate for your esteemed mother-in-law.' She gave me a quizzical look, and I looked away to avoid her penetrating gaze.

'Allesio's message?' I asked again.

'Beware of false friends,' she said with emphasis on the word 'false'. Her look sent a shiver of fear up my spine.

'Gaston, you have made the vilest of enemies in Venerio. He will take his revenge where and with whom he can. Take Allesio's advice and keep a low profile, if you want to live.'

At that point, my appetite took a severe downturn. Any light-hearted attempts at levity on my part almost succeeded, until late evening when Papa and I were alone in his antiquarian garret.

'What did Mama say to upset you?' he asked gravely.

'Papa, why didn't you tell me about your connections to the Faconi family? I would rather have heard it from you than Mama.'

'Our business was concluded years ago, so I saw no need to involve you. Gaston, trust me, you don't want to hear of my past association with that family. They are cruel and merciless; keep them out of your life.'

'That is easier said than done. Guido may be dead, but Inez and Giselle will remain, albeit tenuously, part of their wider family by marriage.'

'Gaston, for the sake of your family, just do as I say.' Papa's head sank into his hands. He looked tired and exasperated by my questioning. Much as I tried to prise more information from him, he would not be drawn and stubbornly refused to listen to any further questions. But he was right. They were both right in their assertions that I must lay low for a while. Of course, this nightmare would end if Vanerio were no longer a living, breathing threat.

Chapter Two

Rising at dawn to the sound of rain beating against Papa's bedroom window did nothing to lift my spirits. My parents' disclosures over dinner the previous evening regarding their knowledge – albeit past knowledge – of the Faconi family continued to occupy my headspace. It made my earlier decision not to tell them of my involvement in Guido's death much easier.

Just then a loud slamming of the front door could be heard, followed by slow labouring footsteps on the stairs, announcing Papa's arrival. His face lit with pleasure as he came into the room.

'Sleep well?' he puffed.

'Sleeping on that bed was like sleeping on top of a wall.'

'Really, that good? I've never had that pleasure,' he chuckled.

'I'm going for a run. Meet you for breakfast in the square in one hour. Same restaurant as last night, got it?'

Papa gave a thumbs-up, then sat down to catch his breath.

The streets were just beginning to fill with shop owners and stall holders preparing for the day's business. The rain became relentless as I slipped into a doorway to check my phone diary. Yes, there it was, 12 noon, meeting a guy going by the weird name of *Volpe*, on a vessel of the same name.

Turning towards the harbour, I slowed to a walk, my eyes searching every berth for *Volpe*. No show yet, but no matter. If the client failed to show, at least I had touched base with my parents.

Before breaking into a run, I dialled Giselle. As expected, there was no reply at this hour. Scrolling through my phone contacts, I found Inez's number. After a few rings, Alex answered.

'Do you know what the time is?' he said sharply.

'Yes, obviously, but more importantly, why are you answering Inez's phone at this hour of the morning?' I replied pointedly.

'My business, so butt out. Anyway, what do you want?' replied Alex tersely.

'I wanted to speak with my mama-in-law, so perhaps you would be good enough to hand her the phone. Presumably she is lying next to you.'

'Absolutely not... unfortunately. She left her phone in the schoolroom kitchen and I am down here prepping breakfast for her students. Now look, mate, I'm busy so is there any message?'

'Just tell her I will be visiting later this week. I need to talk to you both on several matters of concern.'

'Yeah, you're not kidding. I will definitely want to hear your explanation of why you pushed her new husband to his death.'

'Told you earlier to keep your mouth shut, or else I *will* shut it for you.'

'Like to see you try,' said Alex tauntingly.

I pressed the end call button and pocketed my phone. If that guy thought he could dictate to me, he was hugely mistaken. Inez would sort him out; she wouldn't let that joker destroy her only grandson's future.

My run took me out of the town centre through the backstreets, then on to the outer perimeters of the town. As my parents were unlikely to venture no further than 20 metres from their own doorstep, I decided to reconnoitre on their behalf, hoping the prospect of exploring new territory would bring a sense of normality to my chaotic life. After an hour of taking photos, carefully noting artisan food shops and cultural places of interest – and for my own benefit, all roads leading in and out of town, should I need to make a fast exit – my thoughts turned to breakfast, and to Papa waiting in the square. The rain had cleared, leaving a bright clear day, with a prospect of rising early spring temperatures.

Should I take this opportunity to make my confession? Was this the moment, or should I wait to hear Inez's sound advice?

Turning into the square, I found Papa sitting with his arm casually draped around his lady bibliophile friend, their heads close together in animated conversation, like two love-struck doves. I ordered coffee and a *croc madame*. Papa and his friend had already eaten and were absorbed in listing items needed prior to opening his bookshop. I ate quickly, in fact ravenously, and wanted more, but time was short and I needed to speak with Mama alone. Finishing my coffee, I made my excuses then headed straight for a showdown with Mama. She answered the door wearing the same bleak-looking, black trouser suit she had worn the previous day.

'Good morning, Mama, you are still wearing black. Did someone die?' My tone was deliberately flippant.

'Yes, apparently someone did. But then you would know the finer details of the death,' she replied dourly, and for a moment her words failed to register.

'You know the truth.' It was not a question, as she already knew the answer.

'Yes.' She hesitated then opened the door wider. 'You had better come in.'

She stepped aside and gave me a look I will never forget. Her ashen face told me something had happened since our little chat the previous evening.

'Mama, who told you?' I waited expectantly, holding my breath for her answer.

'I'm afraid, Gaston, it was Venerio Faconi himself. He emailed his condolences, as we are about to lose our only son.' She looked at me through reddened eyes, as tears of anguish rolled down her cheeks. 'He will have found my email address on the university's website, so you need to find a place of safety for your family, or find a way to silence him... permanently.'

I walked to the window and looked out to sea, her anguished words circling inside my head.

'Mama, do you really imagine I would allow a low-life thug like him to beat me?'

Grabbing my arm, she shook me forcibly, pinching my arms with her nails.

'Gaston, listen to me. You don't understand. He knows who we are and where we live and he will hound us all into our graves, one by one, until he succeeds. And he will take everything we have, all of us, everything, including your child.'

She looked frightened and utterly defeated. And for the first time in my adult life, I held my mama, distraught and sobbing in my arms. Later, as her sobs subsided, she wiped her face, composed herself, and apologised for her weakness.

'It may be necessary for you and Papa to go away while I sort this mess out.'

She flew at me enraged. 'We would not be in this appalling situation if you had not married into a family of crooks and murderers. Your papa was recently diagnosed with a heart condition. He just doesn't need this additional stress, and neither do I. And hear this, Gaston, we will be staying here. Your papa and I will face whatever life hurls in our direction, together.'

Our brief reconciliation was over; any burgeoning mother-son relationship had now reverted to cruel words and accusations. We sat in stunned silence, drinking strong coffee while attempting to assimilate the enormity of our situation each in our own way, when my phone rang.

'Gaston, where are you? I have been trying to contact you all morning. Giselle is in hospital. The baby is coming early, you must leave immediately. She is asking for you,' implored Flora.

'Tell her I will be with her by late afternoon. There is something I must do before leaving Antibes.'

Mama looked horrified. 'Gaston, you must leave at once, Giselle needs you. Forget this appointment. I will ask your papa to meet these people and explain the situation.'

'No, Mama, the valuation will take half an hour at most, then I will leave for Menton.'

She gave me a look of disgust, then ran upstairs to her office and slammed the door shut.

Chapter Three

At midday, I walked swiftly down to the far end of the harbour where *Volpe* – a strange-looking vessel – swayed at her moorings. She resembled a well-used trading ship rather than a pleasure cruiser, having been painted the stealth shade of mid-grey. Her shiny black fenders hung low on all sides, like cannon balls waiting to be fired – such a contrast to the sleek ocean-going vessels moored alongside her.

Checking the appointment time on my phone gave me the opportunity of considering the questionable taste of my potential client. If he sailed the high seas in this tug-boat, we wouldn't have much in common. The deserted deck was strewn with various pieces of equipment and empty food packets, and the crew had obviously disappeared into the town, intent on buying supplies or lounging drunk in some watering hole while in port. Then, as I stepped aboard and walked towards the doors leading down to the lower deck, strains of music and laughter came floating up from below.

'Hello, hello!' My calls went unanswered.

'Ahoy, anyone there?' I called again, moving further along the deck.

Suddenly the old engines rumbled into life, and a deadly realisation gripped me: this was a trap. Turning sharply with the intention of leaping to safety, the sky darkened as a heavy weight forced me face down onto the deck. I was trapped, held fast in tangle of rope. Struggling, I called out for help, hoping this was some kind of accident, that a mast had split or someone had inadvertently released a trawl net.

Then, to my horror, Venerio appeared from below, waving his fist in the air, shouting to the crew to get underway and out of the harbour. He stared at me, his eyes narrowed to slits, his hand resting on a rope pulley. Instinctively, I reached into my back pocket for my phone, with the intention of warning Alex Forbes that Inez might be the next target.

'Drop the phone, murderer, and empty your pockets,' ordered Venerio curtly.

'Screw you!' I shouted venomously, while pressing every call button.

Venerio took out a gun from inside his coat and pointed it at my head.

'I said, drop the phone,' he snarled menacingly, walking towards me with a look of searing hatred colouring his dark features.

Thrusting my hand through the net, I hurled the phone overboard.

'Screw you, you ugly snake. If you think you'll get away with this, think again, dead man.'

A shot passed my right ear. Obviously he meant business, but I didn't care. One way or another he was going to wind up dead, just like Guido.

'Let me out of here. We can work through this; I have money, lots of money. How much would it take, eh? Come on, be reasonable.'

He scoffed at my suggestion, and any attempt at sounding reasonable fell like a stone into the sea. He knew I would kill him, given half a chance.

'Inez has my cousin Guido's share of the diamonds *and* Palazzo Faconi. She will see sense when I have her daughter and grandson under my control, you'll see. I am not a greedy man. My family's honour rests on the return of what is ours by right.'

'I will be missed,' I told him. 'They will come looking for me, and when they find me, your life will be worthless, as I intend to finish you off myself.'

'Dream on, Gaston. You and your whole family won't be around to witness my death. Now empty your pockets or I will rip them open myself.'

Reluctantly, I fished around in my jean pockets until my hand touched a small penknife kept for emergencies. There was a small hole in the pocket, big enough to push the knife down the hole and into the front seam of my underpants. I considered, wryly, that should the knife open accidentally, I could be joining the ranks of the castrati any time soon. I struggled and made an unsuccessful attempt to stand and defend myself.

Venerio walked over, took aim, then kicked me hard in the stomach. I screamed and doubled up, as a hot, knife-like pain shot through me, while the crew just stood around jeering and laughing.

'Wind the pulley!' Venerio shouted to them. 'If he gets away, you'll all be working down a mineshaft in Africa for the rest of your miserable lives.'

He leaned over me, grinning. 'Don't worry, Gaston, I'm not going to kill you yet. First, you will suffer for murdering Cousin Guido.' He spat in my face, then ordered his crew to hoist me over the side.

'Half drown him, but don't kill him,' he ordered tersely, and watched as they lowered the net into the icy water.

The cold hit me like bullet each time they lowered me deeper and for longer, until I *wanted* to drown, wanted to wash away the stain of guilt and dread of what evil my family might suffer in the future due to my reckless actions.

Finally, after Venerio had had his fun and I was considered subdued enough to be left alone, they secured the net just above the waterline, then left me to marinade in freezing sea-water. The rough net left reddened weals on my bare flesh as I struggled to keep my head above the tide.

Somehow, I had to escape, swim to safety, and warn my family to hide until such time as I could send Venerio Faconi to join his cousin Guido in hell.

As the late afternoon mist rolled over the waves, my head began to feel light and my body feverish, the creeping disorientation of hyperthermia seeped into my brain. Thoughts of Giselle and our child – the child I might never see – floated through my mind as I struggled to hold my breath. The net had sagged, forcing me to choke down more water. Hearing this, the crew hoisted me higher above the wash.

'Don't let him drown!' shouted Venerio to the crew. 'If he drowns, you'll all be next.'

As darkness fell, the weather turned. Waves rising higher than my head crashed into me, battering my body against the side of the boat. I lay still, willing myself not to cry out, not to show weakness, while the salt water penetrated my bleeding wounds. Above the wind, I could hear drunken laughter coming from inside the hull.

Some time later, buckets of hot water were thrown over me, scalding my head and back. I shrank from the scalding water and called for them to stop.

'If he dies, you're all next,' called a slurring Venerio to his crew. 'Watch him. He will not be allowed to die until I have the whole family under my control,' he ordered loudly.

Lying face upwards, hands clasped over my mouth to prevent water penetration, I began to fixate on the brightest stars until vivid hallucinations began forming in my numbed mind. I imagined sharks were circling me and stinging jellyfish clinging to my limbs. Cringing, I screamed out for them to stop, not realising the stings were simply rope cuts. As the night wore on, my frozen, sea-soaked body continued to tremble uncontrollably; rubbing my limbs, in an effort to maintain some circulation, deepened my bleeding sores.

'Am I dead? Is this what death is?' I cried out.

No-one answered my call. There was no sound from the crew. No doubt they were sleeping off their alcohol intake. What I wouldn't have given for a bottle of cognac right now.

The breaking dawn roused me from a stupor. There was no sight nor sound from the crew, and last night's squall had dissipated into calmer waters glistening under the rising sun. Somewhere deep inside me, the will to live flickered in my fragmented mind.

With great effort, I curled into a ball, then worked my numbed fingers down into the place where the knife was hidden. My frozen fingers slipped as the knife opened. *Don't drop the knife; it's your only chance*, I told myself as I began cutting through the rope.

The new knife, a birthday present from Giselle, made short work of the rope and within minutes the hole was large enough for me to slip through unnoticed by the crew, who were probably still suffering with hangovers and lying on their bunks. I waited, not daring to slip through the hole until the cover of nightfall, thereby giving me a better chance of escape.

Occasionally, Venerio would peer over the edge of the boat to check if I was still alive. On each occasion, he spat on me, calling me filthy names.

'Everything you own, your property, the diamonds, even your child, I will take from you, then I will avenge Cousin Guido by killing you myself,' he shouted to me, his lips curled in a sneering grimace.

My body temperature began alternating between shivers and sweats, and the headache – oh, the mind-blowing headache – gave me spiralling double vision.

Desperate to escape, my smarting, salt-encrusted eyes could just make out a distant coastline. Using the sun's position as a compass, I gauged we were heading south along the Italian coast. If Venerio intended making the long voyage home to Venice, I would definitely be dead before we arrived. My only chance of survival was to swim to safety.

'Fetch the man crate!' shouted Vanerio to the crew. 'Bring it here to this side, and make sure he doesn't escape.' His words sent me into a spiral of panic. If they locked me up, it was game over; I had to go – and go now. Suddenly an enormous wave hit the boat, sending bottles and plates rolling around the deck. The crew darted after them in an effort to secure their equipment, while cursing one another for their negligence.

'My friends, you will not get paid if anything is lost, and that includes our prisoner. Hold fast, we're changing course for Genoa, then our murdering Frenchman will be driven overland to Venice.'

Taking the wheel, Venerio unleashed the throttle, forcing the boat to change direction and pick up speed. We were heading out into the open sea.

Decision made, I removed my jeans, let go of the net, then slipped silently through the hole, down into the deep azure waters of the Mediterranean sea, and swam for my life, oblivious to what creatures lay in wait for a substantial meal like me. The strenuous effort of repeated shallow dives began to warm my aching muscles, and swimming semi-submerged to avoid detection gave me a renewed will to survive. When Venerio found the empty net, he would see the hole and know that I had escaped, or been eaten by sharks.

Weak and disoriented from hunger and cold, I made a supreme effort to maintain a straight course towards the coastline. Below the waterline, something nudged my left leg. There it was again. Now my right leg. Terrified there might be sharks around, I swam harder and faster, forcibly pushing myself through the foaming waves. But suddenly overhead there was a rush of air as two dolphins sailed over my head, then swam alongside me, breaching and diving in my path.

I paused momentarily to catch my breath and watch as they performed aerial acrobatics, but treading water in these seas could be deadly. Fixing my eyes on the coastline, I swam as if the devil himself was on my tail.

Hearing engine noise, I turned to see the *Volpe* steering an erratic course, weaving back and forth, presumably searching for me. My lungs felt sodden with exhaustion, making my strokes shorter and increasingly frantic.

As the beach came into view, so the currents changed and my efforts to maintain a direct course became harder. The strong currents started pulling me towards a rocky outcrop, and panic seized me as a vortex of terror flooded my confused mind. Struggling against the turbulence had drained what little energy was left to me, and I began floating, unable to carry on, knowing that at any moment I would be thrown, battered and bleeding, against the treacherous rocks. My life would end here, alone, in these desolate waters.

Looking ahead, I saw a shadowy figure, dressed in flowing black robes, standing calmly on the rocks, watching me impassively. Was this the reaper? Was this where death would claim me, in this place, in a sea I had loved, with birds cawing over my head? If so, my wasted life had meant nothing.

Chapter Four

They told me I was a Frenchman, whose broken body was found by a group of scuba divers, practising deep sea survival techniques. The fingers on my right hand had dislocated while clinging to the rocks, surrounded by sea birds waiting to peck out my eyes and strip my carcass. I had no recollection of my rescue, nor of how long I had lain there in that desolate place. My only recollections were now of what I saw before me.

I was a whispering shell of a man, wracked with pain and drenched in sorrow. They told me I had lain there in that hospital bed for two months, and in my delirium they had fed and cared for this body of which I knew nothing. When alone, I looked down in trepidation at my naked body for evidence of my ordeal and discovered healed scars, still pink and shiny smooth, from injuries sustained as the waves hurled me against the rocks. They told me that the following week would be the beginning of my rehabilitation, physiotherapy, voice coaching, and endless questions about a life that was lost to me.

I am a man lost, dead to myself and afraid of the future. Better that I had died.

Early one glorious summer morning, two purposeful looking medics came without preamble to gather my few belongings, which had been kindly donated by members of hospital staff. They explained that later that day I would be transferred alone by taxi to a rehabilitation hospital near San Remo – a large Italian city close to the French border. The thought of traveling alone to a strange city set my nerves on edge. The hospital would be unfamiliar, winding corridors would seem never-ending, meeting new people would undermine my confidence. I was not ready to enter into discussions with strangers, and as my resentment at being forced out of this place of sanctuary continued to grow, tears of self pity began to flow in torrents, dampening my cast-off shirt and shorts.

A sympathetic male nurse attempted to coax me out of my despair by saying they had done all they could to improve my physical heath, but the time had come for me to learn how to live again. Of course, he was right. Hiding myself away from society would only prolong my reluctance to join a world of which I knew nothing. After making my grateful *adieus* to the staff for saving my life, I departed – albeit reluctantly – with my new jailer.

My journey, a mystical voyage into anonymity, combined a confusing mixture of curiosity and fear of the noisy, congested everyday life now passing before my eyes. I began speculating as to how my future would unfold. Had I lost the capacity to initiate conversations with strangers, or maintain relationships with new friends? What could I tell them of myself when my past life was an empty void? Somewhere in my fragmented mind, I could feel there remained items of unfinished business, dangerous business. Perhaps an insightful medic at the rehabilitation unit would find a way to unlock my head and release me from the empty prison that was my mind.

Clouds of dust rose behind us as we sped out of town. The past few days of sultry heat had given way to overcast skies. Black clouds opened overhead, sending torrents of rain beating down onto the windscreen, while forked lightning pierced the sky as thunder rumbled in the distance. I opened my window to breathe in the electric freshness of cleansed air. Looking out, I saw quaint stone farmhouses surrounded by animal pens, and fields planted with fragrant blue flowers filling the air with their sublime scent. This scent I would remember; this scent would become my new sanctuary.

'What is the name of these flowers?' I asked the driver.

'Monsieur, everyone in France recognises the scent of lavender. After wine, it is our greatest treasure.'

An hour later, we turned into a long drive lined with tall cypress trees, opening out into a formal water garden surrounded by sweeping lawns, bordered by an abundance of exquisitely scented plants. According to my driver, they were roses entwined with clematis. The rehabilitation unit – a white painted villa with pale green shutters – stood in rain-drenched resplendence, its wide verandas with climbing plants swaying over chairs and tables arranged in groups gave the appearance of a smart hotel rather than a hospital.

'Monsieur, you are most fortunate to be staying here in this beautiful place. Here you will regain your manly vigour,' enthused the driver.

Manly vigour was the least of my worries. Right now, my only concern was restoring my memory and getting my life back on track. A feeling of release washed over me as I thanked the driver and watched as he sped off down the drive, leaving me gazing in admiration at my new home. While standing there in this tranquil place, I wondered how long it would take to adapt to my new life.

'Hello and welcome, you must be Gaston,' called a casually dressed young man, wearing an official-looking lanyard. He came forward and introduced himself, saying that he had been assigned to look after me, and if I had any concerns to address them to him.

'Come on, let's sit together for a while and have a drink. I hear your wounds have healed now, so we need to work on your memory. Don't worry, the treatment is laborious but never painful.'

'Glad to hear it. How long will I be staying?'

'As long as it takes, I'm afraid. Most of the staff here live out, so I'll save the introductions until tomorrow,' he said cheerfully.

We sat on the veranda, talking and drinking lager until late evening. He told me something of his life, which was of no interest to me whatsoever. I just wanted to get my memory back and leave as soon as possible.

'Would you mind if we cut this short? My first day out of hospital has left me feeling drained.' This guy was boring the life out of me.

'Fine. The kitchen staff have left a filled baguette in your room. Let's go.'

My room on the first floor had two large windows: one facing east, overlooking the formal gardens at the front of the building, where tall fountains sprayed crystal mountain water into pools planted with lilies; the other to the west, shaded by shutters, had a panorama of gently rising farmland, leading to the distant Alps Maritime.

After unpacking my few belongings, I showered then lay on the bed nibbling nuggets of cheese from the stale baguette. Next morning, I woke late with a hangover.

No-one came to check on me, so I ventured downstairs into the garden, where the other patients had gathered on the terrace to drink coffee and talk – but not to me! They threw glances in my direction, but that was all; obviously I didn't exist. When I had had enough of being ignored, I stood up to leave, with the intention of exploring the grounds.

'Come and meet the staff, then we can make a start,' called the annoying guy who had greeted me on my arrival.

The staff consisted mainly of male nurses, well versed in the business of attending to the feeble-minded. My fellow inmates were, like me, a diverse crowd of vacant-minded souls, awaiting illumination to assail them so they too could resume their previous lives or invent new ones.

He explained the various methods and pathways of my forthcoming treatment.

'They will consist of in-depth consultations, days and possibly weeks of poring over images of towns and cities, people of differing nationalities and types of food and drink. In essence, anything that might prompt your memory. Losing your personal history – as in bereavement – becomes increasingly more traumatic as your physical heath improves. Don't try too hard. Just let your memory evolve naturally through new experiences.'

Sensible thinking, but then he was an expert so I would take him at his word and act accordingly, however boring his sessions became.

At times, tears of rage and disappointment gushed like mountain streams. Nothing seemed real. My memory remained a blank space waiting to be filled with the life I had lost. Maybe it was time to build a new life, rather than waste precious time in futile attempts to step back into the past.

Early one morning, while sitting breathing deeply under a lemon tree, I began to stretch and practise a set of yoga asanas. I have no conception of their origins, only that I know how to perform them, but these exercises would become part of my daily routine, enabling me to gain muscle strength and self-confidence.

Today, my young consultant would accompany me on the first of a series of planned visits into town, exploring the shops and cafés with valuable time spent lounging at street tables, drinking coffee, and all the time watching for any sign –however seemingly inconsequential – of recognition, from lovers whispering and holding hands to families choosing how to spend their day. My consultant had long since ruled out uploading my image onto social media, as doing so might incur criminal interest.

My consultant told me I would face up to six long months trawling art galleries and browsing in book shops, to seek recognition or to build new memories. One hot day, I summoned the courage to face my fear of the sea, by venturing onto the beach. The feeling of warm sand between my toes felt frighteningly familiar in a way that was difficult to explain, but thereafter my morning ritual of yoga practice and beach runs became essential elements in my daily routine. Afternoons were spent helping in the hospital kitchen, as my culinary knowledge and expertise with a chopping knife did not go unnoticed by the staff. They were grateful for my help and paid for my services, which enabled me to travel by public transport to nearby towns and villages, always remembering to make route notes in order to avoid becoming lost.

One glorious mid-summer morning, I decided to relieve my tedium by catching a train to Nice. My consultant gave me a street map and lent me his phone, as a precaution against becoming lost. At the station, I bought a newspaper, intending to relax, people watch in a beachfront café, and absorb the atmosphere in an attempt to convince myself that life really was worth living.

The day passed uneventfully and, as expected, no-one rushed to shake my hand or say hello. Later that afternoon, while walking up to the port, I passed a cluster of stalls selling vintage clothing, various items of furniture, and bric-a-brac. This place, with its bustling crowd of bargain hunters, held my interest. More especially, as the area seemed vaguely familiar to me, I wondered if sometime in the future maybe this could be my type of business.

Feeling thirsty, I retraced my steps. The route drew me into the historic district and busy market place, surrounded by restaurants and potential diners, all comparing menus posted on stands along the pavements. A growing feeling of elation took hold of me as I walked past the opera house. *I know this place*, I thought. *This place is home.* And for the first time in months, a thrilling resurgence of hope flooded my entire body.

Until recently, my only human contact had been confined to fellow male patients, most of whom had repelled my repeated attempts at conversation and appeared to regard me with blatant suspicion. The time-starved medics and kitchen staff were friendly enough, but now, since the revelatory visit to Nice, my horizons had expanded. My time in this beautiful, safe place would shortly come to an end. Soon the authorities would consider me able to cope with the outside world and would make plans and, far worse, decisions regarding my future.

Naturally, amnesia had some dubious advantages, such as a total exoneration for any past misdemeanours, acts of callus cruelty, and the cultivation of nefarious associates.

Having severely limited personal funds to draw on was becoming an annoying impediment to my recovery, and after pleading for extra hours in the hospital kitchen, I decided the best course of action would be to apply for a position as a waiter at a decent restaurant in town.

Next morning, I rose at dawn and made my way to the kitchens, intending to prepare breakfast for the staff and residents. No menus meant no prep, so I took an orange from the fruit bowl, then slipped out into the garden to stretch my legs and practise a few asanas. The garden was quiet and still on that windless summer morning, and potent scents of roses and honeysuckle came wafting in my direction to suffuse my senses and quieten my mind while I lay stretched out on the grass, luxuriating in the sun's warmth, with butterflies hovering around my bare toes. The ripe orange in my hand felt soft and yielding in my palm. Lifting the peel, I imagined myself gently removing my lover's clothing. Gently, my fingers segmented then sucked the luscious fruit until my appetite felt satiated. This was my moment of acceptance and of decision to leave this place of refuge, my haven of peace these past months. I was not meant to live a half-life.

Somewhere beyond this place were disconnected threads of my previous life. But how could I move on without first resolving the past?

Later that afternoon, freshly showered and dressed in cast-off clothes donated by the hospital kitchen staff, I hitched a lift into town. I intended to get a haircut, then trawl the smarter restaurants in the hope of being hired for the remaining summer season. The first three eateries were non-starters, as their menus consisted mainly of poorly presented, barely palatable, fast food. Feeling thirsty, I headed for a beach-front café serving wood-fired pizza, seafood risottos, and an impressive selection of fresh, locally grown salads.

The afternoon had turned hot and humid. Above the waves, a filmy heat haze merged sea and sky, and yet again I speculated as to what had happened to me in those deep, dark waters. The sun-drenched beach was almost deserted, except for a few brave sun-loving tourists working on their tans. At siesta time, acclimatised locals completely avoided the midday heat by lunching in the shade, then stealing away for a power-nap before emerging later, refreshed and ready for their evening's occupation or entertainment. Feeling relaxed, I chose a shady corner in which to sit and enjoy the scenery, while waiting for the nice-looking waitress with stunning legs to glide over and take my order.

'*Bonjour, mademoiselle*, nice place you have here. Can I have a beer and a job, please?' She laughed in surprise. In my experience, people rarely refuse polite requests.

'A beer certainly, *monsieur*, a job… maybe more difficult. The manager will be here later, so leave your phone number and he'll call you if we have a vacancy,' she said smiling, pencil raised ready to take my non-existent phone number.

'I'll be here for while,' I replied. 'Maybe he'll show before I leave.'

Phew, side-stepped that one! How could anyone admit to not having a mobile phone number?

After finishing my beer, I ordered another, along with a dish of risotto. When the waitress returned with my drink, she told me the boss had arrived and would join me when I had finished my meal. Some 20 minutes later, a guy came striding towards me.

Suddenly, he came to an abrupt halt, staring wide-eyed in disbelief, as if he'd seen a spirit.

'Gaston, is it really you? They told me you were dead. No-one knew what had happened to you! Where did you go?'

I looked at him in astonishment. *He called me Gaston; he knows me; he knows my friends.*

His initial surprise quickly turned to irritation, as I sat dumbfounded and unable to answer him.

'Look, Gaston, I don't know what mischief you've been up to, but if it's another woman, you should go back to Menton, come clean and tell Giselle. Why have you come here asking for a job when you have a café of your own? For God's sake, man, what is going on?' He lit a cigarette then leaned back in his chair. 'Well, come on then, let's hear it, and it better be good.' His belligerent attitude left me feeling somewhat defensive. What could I tell him?

'Gaston, speak to me. Are you ill?' he pressed on irritably.

'Sorry, my friend, but I don't know you, or anyone. However, what I do know is that I was found roughly six months ago by a group of scuba divers, close to death, clinging to rocks off Cap d'Antibes. After a long sojourn in hospital, they transferred me to a rehab unit near here and are still treating me for amnesia.' The nameless antagonist sitting opposite took a few minutes to assimilate my words.

'Yeah well, Gaston, it's a good story, best yet... So, prove it. Let's say I take you back to this so-called rehab unit, one that I have never heard of, right now.'

'Fine, let's go,' I said stiffly. *If he thinks I'm lying, he's in for a surprise.*

As we stood up to leave, he frowned and offered me his hand. 'Gaston, I can see by your expression that you don't remember me. I am Jules Abreo, a lifelong friend.'

Apart from giving Jules directions, neither of us spoke on our journey out of the city. My mind fizzed with anticipation; this man said I had a wife living in Menton, and a café. He seemed to know so much about my lost life – a life that thankfully was about to be resumed.

Arriving at the rehab unit, I asked to see my consultant. Unfortunately, he was unavailable for the day, so another member of staff, not assigned to my welfare, collected my notes and took his place. In the privacy of my room, and with my permission, we openly discussed my case. The medic confirmed the details of my conversation with Jules earlier that day.

'Look here, Gaston, I owe you a profound apology,' said Jules, his face a study of concern. 'After such an horrific accident, little wonder you've lost your head.'

'Not quite lost, simply misplaced,' said the medic firmly.

Later that evening, Jules fetched a bottle of cognac from his car and we sat in the lemon grove, drowsing and drinking by candlelight until a new dawn rose over our heads. It was a new dawn for me, as Jules had spent the whole night recounting the highs and emphasising the lows of my past life with such clarity that parts left me feeling either shocked or rolling around with laughter.

Next morning, feeling dishevelled and hungover, I made Jules promise not to contact my family; it was too soon. I was not ready to face the trauma of accusations and disbelief. Not now; not even next week. But now, as he reminded me, I had a choice. I could leave and never, ever look back, as this would be my one and only chance to escape the Roxberg taint which Giselle's family had brought upon me. But now, there was my son Luc to consider. Could I leave him? Never.

Chapter Five

One week later, I found the courage to make two phone calls: one to Jules, asking if he would accompany me to Menton; the other to my café, booking a table for the following day, in the name of Gaston Villande.

'So what kind of sick joke would you be playing then?' came the terse response.

'Am I speaking to Iona?'

'Who else? Is that Gaston?' she retorted sharply.

'Yes, Iona. I had an accident, resulting in memory loss.' She dropped the phone then called out, 'Gaston's alive! He's coming home!'

Returning to the phone, she went on, 'So what happened? Cheek of it, leaving us here to cope. Where did ye go?' As an employee left to cope with a busy café; obviously she felt she had every right to demand answers to her barrage of questions. Questions that for the moment were none of her business.

'Iona, is my wife at home?'

'Ye have no wife; she divorced ye. Gone to Paris with her fancy man. Left the bairn with Inez.'

The surprise of hearing from an employee that my marital status had taken a downward turn left me feeling emotionless and vaguely relieved.

'Iona, listen to me. Please ring Inez. Tell her I am suffering from amnesia, as a result of an accident, and also that I will collect Luc at some point over the next few days, after familiarising myself at home.'

'Ye'll need a car then; it was stolen just after ye left Antibes. *And* ye'll need to bring that au pair back with ye. I'm too busy running this place to care for a bairn, and Flora is no nursery maid. I need her here with me,' she interjected loudly.

'Iona, please calm yourself. Tomorrow you will have an extra pair of hands. We can talk then. *Au revoir.*'

I was relieved to hear Iona' demanding voice. At the very least there was still a business to return to. If she had been running the café pretty much single-handed in my absence, whatever happened, she would be first in line for a substantial bonus, with paid holiday.

The news of Giselle's decision to divorce me circled in my mind. A surprise, yes, but not one that was particularly unpleasing, as I still had no clear recollection of our life together. It was feasible that a divorce had already been on the horizon prior to my accident.

Ascertaining my financial position should present no difficulties, as presumably my passport and other identity documents should be where they were stored prior to my accident. But I would need a car and a phone.

My first priority, however, was the return of my son. Hopefully, Inez and Giselle would not object, as any attempt to undermine my credibility as a father would result in a fierce battle through the courts. Giselle had abandoned our son and therefore, in my opinion, a judge would consider her unfit to raise a child.

Next morning, before Jules arrived, having signed my release papers and made grateful *adieus* to the staff, I called my parents.

Afterwards, I sat in the lemon grove impatiently drumming my fingers on the seat, willing Jules to arrive, impatient to resume a life that was beyond my knowledge or understanding. After a seemingly interminable hour, he arrived, all smiles and affability.

'Been waiting long, Gaston?' he remarked cheekily.

'Yes, Jules, six months. Now, let's leave.'

The boot of his red two-seater swallowed up my few belongings without any difficulty. As we drove away, I glanced back at the beautiful house that had saved my sanity over the last six months, standing serenely, shaded from the midday sun by an immense cedar. My eyes welled with emotional gratitude as I sobbed uncontrollably until we reached the outskirts of Menton.

'You're still strung out,' said Jules, looking concerned. 'Coming home and immersing yourself in the business will be your best therapy. Inez will soon sort you out, and there's your son. God, I wish I had a son,' said Jules wistfully.

'Obviously, you haven't heard.'

He turned to me with raised eyebrows. 'What now? Not again, not more dramas. Gaston, your life is a living nightmare, and I have known you long enough to have heard the whole sorry tale.'

'Oh thanks... still, it beats being a dull bore like you.' We laughed like old comrades reminiscing in the aftermath of war. Or was this just the beginning of my new war?

'Well, listen to this. Iona informed me, in her usual forthright manner, that Giselle has left Menton and has not only taken a permanent post at a prestigious gallery in Paris, but is living with one of its directors in Montmartre. And even more interesting, Iona said she has divorced me in my absence and without my consent. Is that possible, or even legal?' I said with incredulous amusement.

Jules gave me a sidelong glance, his thoughtful look settling into a frown. 'You don't seem mightily concerned about losing Giselle or her inheritance.'

'All I care about is having a viable business and the safety of my son. If Giselle wants to cut loose, then let her. I don't want a woman who doesn't want me and, let's face it, I have absolutely no recollection of her, or her family.'

But, of course, some of that was now untrue. Since speaking with Iona, my splintered memory had begun making vivid, unconnected images in my nightmares.

We arrived in sun-drenched Menton just as the lunchtime service had begun.

My first glimpse of the café, as we drove along the tree-lined street, was of a tall building, with pale blue and white striped awnings positioned over the outside seating areas and of louvred window shutters painted in a similar hue to match the front door. We sat momentarily absorbing the scene of tables covered with spotless, blue checked cloths. Blue glass jugs, containing posies of vanilla-scented heliotrope, stood as centrepieces on each table. Windows sparkled in the midday sun as a young girl stood taking an order, severe in her flowing, black linen dress. We sat, lost in admiration, as she moved between the tables, the side vents in her dress revealing tantalising glimpses of her long, tanned limbs as she walked.

'If you're thinking what I'm thinking, we could both be arrested,' remarked Jules, openly leering at the waitress.

'Hey, get down, she's young enough to be your daughter.'

'Well, if you ever need extra staff, let me know,' he said lavishly.

'Right, let's go. *You* are my only witness, and I have some explaining to do.'

As the car doors slammed shut, the waitress turned her head, and my beating heart lurched against my ribs.

'Gaston! Oh Gaston,' she shrieked, 'is it really you? Oh my life, it really is you. Thank God, you're alive.'

She ran into my arms, tears streaming down her cheeks, while customers ceased talking to enjoy the moment. Suddenly, the kitchen door burst open and a female with pale, braided hair, wearing a ferocious expression, rushed towards me brandishing a wooden spoon and cracked me on the elbow. We all stood transfixed to the spot, a tableau of fearful expectation, waiting for someone to make the next move.

'Look at ye, thin as water,' she said, pointing the spoon in my direction, rather like a truncheon. 'A ball-n-chain, that's what ye need to stop ye wandering,' she continued huffily. 'Well, ye here now. Lunch is ready, so don't be dawdling. And what are ye doing here, Jules?'

So it was true; he was a genuine friend from my past.

'I am here, Iona, to confirm Gaston's account of his recent misfortunes, so you can put that weapon in the kitchen drawer where it belongs.'

'Perhaps we should go indoors, and Flora, please write a notice for the door, saying we are closing for three weeks. Time now for you and Iona to enjoy a well-earned rest... with full pay, naturally. And time also for me to familiarise myself here without Iona's acerbic commentary.'

After Jules had initially enlightened me about my ownership of a café, I had spent time lounging in the sun, imagining my café to be a smoky, seductive bistro, when in reality the décor was more froufrou light and fresh colour scheme, similar to the exterior.

'Hard to believe ye don't know this place,' remarked Iona, suspicion written large on her Nordic features. She bustled around the kitchen like an egg-bound hen, tutting while refusing help and pushing us out of her path. 'There's chairs in the dining room, be advised to use them.' We all rolled our eyes then moved to a safe distance.

'Iona, you don't seem pleased to see me home and safe, if not a little unsound.'

She pouted, adjusted her apron, and gave me a belligerent look while remaining uncompromisingly obtuse.

'We're having ye favourite lobster with a caviar dressing, green salad with kiwi, olives and avocado, just how you like it,' she said firmly, her eyes bright with satisfied defiance.

'Thank you, Iona. Can I assume that's a yes, and that you are pleased to see me, so we can expect no unpleasantness now, or in the future?'

Silence.

'Well, Gaston, at least *I* am so, so happy to see you again,' enthused Flora.

Iona turned on her sharply. 'Ye are not old enough to be liking a man twice you're age, my girl.' She glared at the young girl.

'Now, for dessert we're having chocolate pots. Just how you like them – laced with lime compote, crushed pistachios, and your very best champagne,' announced

Iona loudly. 'And if you can't remember that, you can't remember anything,' she bellowed, pointing her weapon of choice in my direction.

At this, my patience began to waver.

'Iona, I do not recognise you, your food, or this building, but let *me* give *you* some sound advice. Until either my memory or my sense of humour returns, be good enough to show me, *your* employer, a little respect if you want our association to continue. Now, let's begin again on a more convivial note.'

Iona gave me a darkling look, then set about noisily laying the table. There followed a flurry of snowy damask, the clashing of silver cutlery, a clinking of crystal then finally, she dumped a huge silver ice bucket containing three bottles of champagne as a centrepiece, surrounded by a bouquet of yellow roses.

Cracking open the first bottle, we raised our glasses to toast Flora and Iona for their loyalty and hard work in keeping the café open in my long absence.

Lunch was a triumph of subtle flavours. Every delicious mouthful uplifted my tastebuds after having endured the mediocrity of institutional cuisine. Iona and Flora listened intently as Jules recounted his version of my life since entering rehab, his words painting an odyssey of truth and lies, my life in pictures on the blank canvas that is my mind.

Chapter Six

Later that evening, after Jules and Iona had departed, Flora – in a state of euphoric inebriation – had been safely escorted downstairs to the flat she shared with 'Thing', a stray terrier found wandering the beach some seven months ago. I decided to investigate the other rooms in my three-storey house. Café Villande occupied most of the ground floor, leaving space for what appeared to be my cramped office. Someone with a head for figures had meticulously kept an invoice diary, with paper invoices filed in date order, awaiting entry onto the computer system.

My top floor suite consisted of a petite salon, furnished in a contemporary minimalist style in various shades of blue, with doors opening onto a full-width, white filigree metal balcony. The large bedroom had been aired and the en-suite bathroom shelves filled with unopened vetiver-scented toiletries, left by someone more familiar with my preferences than myself. A walk-in-wardrobe, overcrowded with masses of casually elegant garments waiting to be reunited with their owner, hung on rails reeking of mothballs. And musty, ripe-smelling shoes languished on racks in the airless summer heat.

Looking around, I felt the absence of recognition or any sense of belonging. This room, this house, this life were like open wounds unable to heal; voids of emptiness where memories refused to gather, like a sea shell buffeted against the waves of a life yet to be remembered.

Taking a full measure of cognac out onto the balcony, intending to sit and watch the sun's rays painting the sky with fingers of crimson, I began speculating as to Giselle's reaction on hearing of my survival. Would she regret moving on so rapidly and callously abandoning our child? Or would she be relieved to be free to follow her career and start again with a man old enough to be her father? That and more would be revealed over the coming weeks. And what of innocent, uncomplicated Flora? She will love my son, and in return, I will make myself love her, if she feels any attachment to me.

Dismissing my melancholic thoughts, I finished my cognac, headed for the shower and then to bed. Someone had sprinkled drops of lavender on cool cotton sheets, and the seductive combination of alcohol and essential oil induced a blissful drowsiness. As my head touched the pillow, I fell into a fitful, sexually frustrated sleep. Erotic visions of Flora dressed in flowing gossamer silk, rising from the waves, calling to me to join her, passed back and forth through my mind as I slept on.

'Come to me, Gaston, I need you. What are you waiting for?' she called as I waded out to her. But as I drew closer, her face dissolved and was replaced by a black hood with a beckoning hand. Then, as a miasma of terror crept up my spine, I cried out, and woke drenched in perspiration. Answers, surely soon there *would* be answers.

As dawn broke, I staggered into the bathroom, still feeling sexually frustrated, and relying on a cold shower to kick-start the day.

My habitual early morning routine, adopted while in rehab, had lingered on. First a run, followed by a cool shower, then yoga practice, and finally, an espresso together with a cappuccino. But not today. Today marked the beginning of my new life – a life where I called the shots and answered to no-one.

Filling the coffee machine with water and inserting a pod, I went out onto the balcony with the intention of compiling a to-do list for the day. The cool morning air had left traces of mist over the waves. I shuddered, remembering the black hood and gloved hand seen so vividly in my nightmare. Sitting , frankly, wallowing in morbid introspection, my attention was drawn to the distant sound of a dog barking so incessantly that I drank my espresso in one gulp and went in search of the animal.

Firstly, I checked the suite below mine, which apparently had belonged to Giselle. It was now completely empty, as she had taken the furniture, along with her affections, to her new life in Paris.

The frenetic barking seemed to emanate from the cellar. Then I remembered Flora's little terrier. Thinking Flora might have had an accident or started a fire, I raced outside, down a flight of steep steps to the basement, and hammered on the door. After a few minutes, she appeared looking distinctly hungover. The shock of seeing her wearing a gossamer nightdress, almost identical to the one seen in my nightmare, momentarily took my breath.

'Oh Gaston, my head is exploding. *Please*, would you take Thing for a walk and give him breakfast?' The dog whimpered and eyed me expectantly.

'Ok, here's the deal. I will walk your mutt, then we can all have breakfast together.'

She looked up in surprise. 'Oh, so you don't mind him being in your kitchen? You always used to mind.'

'Who said anything about my kitchen? We can have breakfast at the beach. See you in a couple of hours.'

I gave the dog my apple, then waited while he acquainted himself with the nearest lamp post and very nearly my bare leg.

'Come on, mutt,' I called, breaking into a run.

He hesitated and kept looking in the direction of home, but after a few minutes of indecision he got the message and came racing down the seafront after me. After half a kilometre, he sat down, refused to go on, and began barking loudly, presumably asking to be carried. I put him across my shoulder and went in search of a phone shop.

En route, I passed a couple sitting out eating croissants and drinking black coffee. They immediately recognised me and called out, 'Hey, Gaston, we heard you are now a single man, and that Giselle has taken a lover.'

Feeling stung by their comments, I took a wrong turn and became completely lost. I hoped Thing knew his way home. Once grounded, he shot off, with me on his tail, running hard to keep up.

As the café came into view, I saw an old jeep parked in my space. Nearby, an attractive female paced back and forth, talking into her phone, while a guy dressed in yellow shorts and t-shirt stood with his finger permanently pressed on my doorbell, waiting to be admitted. Coming to a swift halt, I stood watching. *This looks like trouble* , I thought, hoping the closed sign would encourage them to leave.

I was about to succumb to an overwhelming temptation to turn and run when they saw me and came running towards me, waving and shouting loudly.

'Where are they, Gaston? Where are Luc and Aria?' screamed the flame-haired virago so intent on shattering my nerves. This could only be Inez and her companion, Alex Forbes. My mystified expression should have told them everything.

They can think twice before attempting to harangue me, I thought militantly.

'Whose asking?' I asked insolently.

'Come on, Gaston, you know who we are, so stop wasting our time. We are referring to your son's disappearance. Where is he?'

'My son is in your care, so I would ask you the same question. And if anything of a serious nature has happened to him, I will personally hang you both from the nearest tree. You, Inez, are responsible for Luc's safety.'

'Oh yes, and what would you know about responsibility, given your track record?' retorted Alex.

'Look, Alex, presuming you are Alex, I don't have to take this from you.'

'Yes, you do, and shortly I am going to show you why. You will do exactly as I say, if you know what's good for you.'

'Stop it. Stop it, both of you now, this minute!' screamed Inez, stamping her foot in anger. 'These pointless arguments won't bring Luc back... Oh my God, what if he is already dead?' She turned her stricken face to me.

'So who is this Aria, and what connection does she have to my son?' I snapped.

'She turned up on our doorstep at *Maison des Artistes*, looking for a job. Initially, she was assigned dining room duties, but it soon transpired that she was better placed to care for Luc. He loved her, and she kept him occupied while we attended to our pupils. Her unusual beauty appealed to the students, and occasionally she would agree to model for us. Now we suspect she was a spy sent by Venerio Faconi, a distant cousin of mine by marriage.

'Be assured, Gaston, we will rescue Luc. Venerio can have my money and that rotting Venetian palazzo, as long as no harm comes to Luc. And Gaston...' she paused, searching my face, willing me to remember her, 'Gaston, we are certain Venerio was responsible for your accident. Iona has told us of your traumatic episode and she has accepted your loss of memory is genuine, but I cannot accept your word without irrefutable evidence, given your past.

'Let's face it, Gaston, you are a troublemaker. Bad luck follows you around. So for now, our differences will be ignored, and this in-fighting between you Alex must cease until we have rescued Luc. Then, and only then, we will decide your fate, but now we must wait for Venerio to contact us with a ransom demand.' She turned away, her eyes filling with tears.

'You can wait, but he has my son, so I am going put that bastard where he belongs... in a box. As to my fate, my fate is mine to choose, as you will play no part in it.'

'It's not safe out here. Let's go inside. And you, Gaston, are not safe anywhere,' said Alex reproachfully.

Suddenly Flora put her head out of a window, calling hello to Inez and Alex, then asked if we were still meeting for our walk.

'Sorry, Flora, maybe later. We have business to discuss.'

'Ok, Gaston. Call me.'

'Didn't take you long to find Giselle's replacement,' remarked Alex nastily.

'Will you two cease bickering! And please, Gaston, where are your door keys?'

While I made coffee, they sat in my office with the door shut. I could hear raised voices and wondered if their relationship had buckled under the strain of losing my son, but nothing prepared me for the revelations to come.

'Ok, so firstly, I have something here you need to watch.' Alex handed me his phone, and as I watched the unfolding horror of my act of revenge in pushing Guido Faconi to his death, I felt nothing except burning resentment.

'Perhaps you would care to expand on this concoction of pure fiction.' *This is not happening,* I told myself. *I will not allow these people to damage my life again; it's, time to be rid of them all.*

'Gaston, it's not fiction. You pushed my late husband to his death, in an act of revenge to save our family from destruction. Informing the authorities is not an option, as they may launch further investigations, then who knows where it will lead.'

Alex nodded his agreement. 'Inez is right. We don't want any inquisitive gendarmes delving into our private family business.'

'You're not family, so save your opinions for someone who gives a damn. Of course, you could be lying in order to trick me into disposing of Venerio. For all I know, Luc may be at Villefranche, tucked up his cot.'

'Gaston, have you ever known me to lie to you? We know what Venerio wants – my diamonds and your neck – and he will drive us into our graves unless we stop him… and we mean permanently.'

'Oh, so let me get this straight. Are you asking me to kill this guy for you?'

'Having murdered once, you have nothing to lose by killing again. It's quite simple, Venerio has your son. Your mess, you clean it up. I have former colleagues who will provide back-up, at a price,' remarked Alex convincingly. Inez covered her ears.

'Please do not speak of this proposed atrocity in my hearing,' she interrupted, waving her hand to clear the air. 'Luc will be safe with Aria; she is accustomed to his routines,' she said, searching her bag for a large envelope containing images of Luc. The resemblance was clear, the images almost identical to that of my younger self. She watched intently as I gazed at the images of my son, her eyes searching my anguished face.

'We were such good friends, you and I, but somehow your proclivity for, shall we say… risky escapades, would inevitably become your downfall. And ours, too, if we continue our association.'

Alex sat listening intently, a self-satisfied smile playing about his lips on hearing our heated exchange.

I gave him a sneering glance. *One day, my friend. One day, it will be your turn to involve yourself in the dangerous complexities of Roxberg business,* I thought. *Then we shall see who will be the loser.*

'So, everything is my fault. My fault that you, not once, but twice, married into the criminal underworld, then expected me to redeem the situation. What the hell did you expect me to do, stand by and allow these people to steal your wealth, everything your parents worked their whole lives for? No, it's not happening. Not now, not ever.'

'Gaston, I have always loved you as a son – or even as a potential lover, had Giselle's self-obsession become too demanding. She was bereft when you disappeared, wrongly assuming you were not ready to deal with the rigours of parenthood and had taken the easy route out of her life. Gaston, we can resolve this dreadful situation together.' She turned her green eyes towards me.

'Please, Gaston. None of us are safe while Venerio lives. We are staying at a hotel in Nice for a few days to make plans. Giselle will join us tomorrow, then we can talk. I see the café is closed for a while. Good, as you will be required to take a short trip to Venice.'

'Fine, take my new mobile number and leave me to think this through.'

Alex eyed me suspiciously.

'And, Gaston, don't think about going it alone,' he snapped. 'Venerio can out-run you any time. You will be dead meat as soon as he has the diamonds. Until tomorrow, sleep well.'

Sleep well, he said; I might never sleep again.

'And you can swallow your sarcasm, if you want my help,' I replied.

Alex just laughed. The guy is still a joker. *Still a joker... how did I remember that?*

Some events were best forgotten, and my alleged attack on Guido Faconi was one of them. Naturally, Inez's biased version of life, prior to my accident, could not entirely be trusted. But then, who could I trust? Myself, and perhaps one other.

Chapter Seven

After a quick shower and a vodka shot, I went in search of Flora, thinking she might be persuaded to reveal all she remembered of my life before the accident. Her version of events, from a female perspective, might begin to unlock the mystery and subterfuge impeding my progress to normality. Although my physical strength had returned, the voids in my memory were beginning to cloud my judgement. I needed someone to transport my mind to a happier place, and Flora had become my preferred mode of transport.

She opened the door, wearing a short summer dress, her unruly curls blowing gently in the warm sea breezes. Her air of disarming fragility caught me off balance.

'Hi, are you ready for lunch?' I asked casually.

'We need to walk Thing first, or he might disgrace himself,' she giggled and went indoors to find her sun hat and a dog lead.

Popping my head in, I noted the tiny bedsit had been well fitted out with cupboards and shelves, but nowhere to cook or store food.

'So, how do you live without a kitchen? Presumably you have an en-suite?'

She looked at me and nodded. 'No problem. I have a key to the café. Giselle and Iona both agreed my salary includes dishes from our café menu. This space allows me privacy and a place to study. Shall we walk, or would you like a guided tour? It will only take a minute.'

I got the message loud and clear; perhaps this young woman was not as fragile as she appeared.

Setting off along the seafront, as we walked my thoughts kept returning to Alex's video footage. Suppose it was fake, a ploy, their plan to trick me into murdering Venerio. It would be very neat and convenient for them, but I had my own reasons for wanting him dead. As yet, there had been no contact or ransom demand, so how could I be sure Luc was anywhere other than at home in Villefranche, sound asleep in the arms of the au pair.

After a while, Thing sat and stubbornly refused to go on without the incentive of numerous treats. After half an hour of coaxing, we gave in and sipped takeaway coffee on a street bench – not the most conducive of settings for plying information from a romantically inclined teenager, but I had to try.

'So, Flora, tell me something of your life. And please begin as far back as you can remember, starting with your age.'

She gave me a wounded look. 'Gaston, please don't patronise me. I am not a child, and if you think of me as a silly virgin, you're wrong, because my butterfly lost its wings years ago at school.

'I will be 18 next month – old enough for anything. And if you really want to re-visit the horrors of Roxberg Gate, ask Iona. She knows everything,' she chided.

'Ok, ok. Please accept my apology, and yes, my interest is genuine but entirely selfish. I was hoping you might help rearrange my jigsaw puzzle of a life before the accident stole my memory.'

'Fine, so long as you won't pity me. I don't like being pitied. It makes me feel angry and vulnerable, so no sympathy, promise.' She lifted her chin and turned her gaze to the rolling waves crashing on the shoreline.

'Promise. And, Flora, I absolutely would love to hear about your life. So let's find a restaurant then you can torch me in comfort.'

She slipped her soft hand into mine. 'Deal. Come on then, old thing. I am famished.'

Old thing? Indeed I am not, I thought. *As she may soon discover.*

We walked to the far end of town. Thing's legs kept giving out, and he began pawing my bare legs, asking to be carried. After a while, I caved in and placed him astride my shoulder. There he stayed, panting in my ear until we found a quiet spot to eat outdoors. Soon we found a secluded bistro on the edge of town, with a secluded table under a bougainvillea-clad pergola.

This place is perfect for some gentle interrogation, I thought wryly.

After a lengthy wait, an inattentive waiter approached at a leisurely pace, wearing an insolent expression of disapproval which immediately set my temper soaring. While proffering handwritten menus in our general direction, he smiled at Flora and made a sad face.

This guy was getting closer to being hauled in front of the owner or receiving a serious put-down from me if his attitude failed to improve. No doubt he was assessing our relationship; as if it was any of his damn business whether we were father and daughter, or that I was just another hopeful sugar-daddy chancing his luck.

'Shall we leave before you completely lose it?' said Flora in ringing tones. 'But if you prefer to stay, I will have fish and fries.'

Hearing this, the guy retreated, saying the drinks waiter would be with us shortly. And now, after experiencing first-hand the jealousy of unattractive men unable to excite a woman, I sat wondering if every couple of vastly differing ages received the same outdated reaction from everyone they met. And if so, Flora – however tempting – was not for me.

The weather had unexpectedly turned fresh and invigorating, we relaxed in our shady spot, then ordered crab salad, French fries, and a bottle of Chablis. Was that a wise move? I didn't care. If Flora wanted a glass of wine, then why not?

Throughout our meal, Flora sipped from my glass and regaled me with her educational aims and ambitions – a stark reminder for me of her tender years.

'So, tell me, have you plans after university?' I held my breath.

'Oh yes, no university. I'm staying here with you and Luc. We can have fun making babies, and when you're really old, I will push your wheelchair.'

'Well, that sounds like a very good plan. Do I have any say in this?'

'None whatsoever,' she replied in all seriousness.

'Dessert?' I enquired breathlessly.

'We could substitute dessert for making love.' Her eyes held mine with a blatant intensity.

'Not sure the management would approve, *and* the table is too small.'

We fell about laughing, and for the first time in a long time, I felt the glow of pure unaffected joy.

'Gaston, please listen to me. I have loved you from the moment we first met in the garden at Roxberg Gate. My God... then I was a mere child, and you, you were the archetypal arty type, living in the moment, loving life. And now look what Giselle's family have done to you. You are a fading shadow of your former self. You must end this farce if we are to be happy.'

I wanted to tell her, to show her what happened in Villefranche on the day when Guido lost his life. I wanted more than ever to exonerate myself from blame, but now my courage had failed me. But then, maybe I was getting ahead of myself, presuming too much by looking too far into the future, a future that could at any moment be destroyed by the past.

We sat nibbling a shared starter of warm camembert, spread thickly on garlic toast, and drank wine and delighted in each other's company.

'Why was it necessary for you to live with Iona? Were there no other relatives to care for you? Merely a tentative enquiry, you understand. No pressure.'

She hesitated for a few moments, as if recounting her early life would be too painful an experience to share. Then she sighed, her eyes focusing on the distant horizon.

'My parents and Iona were close friends and neighbours. One blustery autumn night, they went out to a harvest dance, and were killed in a car accident on the way home. I was just 12 years old. Iona is my godmother, and she was childless and, in those days, resolutely single. She immediately stepped into my parents' shoes, becoming a substitute mother, and a brilliant one at that.

'I remember those long hot summers of my childhood. In the school holidays, Iona would take me with her to Roxberg Gate to play with Honore and Simone.

They were children of the house, untouchable, never at fault; no-one dared mention their complicated parentage and unorthodox way of life. Simone had evil ways like her mother and she teased me mercilessly, always calling me the cook's orphan. I hated her for it and we fought like cats, but Honore was so different, so generous and caring. She would dry my tears and share her sweets. Then she grew up and died in the avalanche, then everything changed. I cried for weeks and still miss her gentle smile.

'Oh yes, and Iona told me all about Margot, Henry Roxberg's weird housekeeper, and how he allowed her to poison anyone who crossed her. Iona said she gave him potions to turn him on. She didn't need them, as the old witch was stunningly beautiful.

'It's only since moving to France that Giselle and I have become friends. As children, we hardly ever saw each other, because she lived with Inez at Honfleur. Iona is convinced Roxberg Gate is haunted by the evil spirits of past inhabitants. They have tainted the whole family, and now they have tainted you. Please, Gaston, allow me peel back those tainted layers before it's too late.' She hesitated, her magnetic hazel eyes searching my face for signs of affection or lust.

'Flora, you flatter me, and I am grateful, but there is something I must do. Something so terrifying, so indescribably vile, I hardly dare think of it.'

'Yes, I overheard part of your conversation with Inez and Alex. We must be together tonight before you leave for Venice, or like Giselle, will I be forced to sit and wait, not knowing if you are alive or dead?'

The innocence of our burgeoning relationship was lost forever, drowned without trace in the detritus of my chaotic life. Would Flora become my safe haven, my path to redemption, or merely a transient diversion from approaching danger?

After lunch, we parted – a tense, expectant parting, as neither of us had the slightest conception of where our relationship, if any, might lead. Yes, she was young and of an age when frenetic sexual indulgences were commonplace, as opposed to my preference for sensual tantric rituals. But finding ourselves sexually mismatched would be disastrous for her and inconvenient for me, as the smooth running of the café and the wellbeing of my son depended on her cooperation. And I couldn't forget Iona, who would definitely have strong opinions on the matter. So, with some reluctance, I decided to walk her home, tether my impulses, have a few drinks, and go through the café accounts.

Taking my laptop onto the balcony, I lay listening as foaming waves pounded the shore, driven by a strengthening westerly breeze, filling the air with grains of acrid salt. At midnight, the phone in my office began ringing. At that hour, it could only mean one thing... trouble.

'Switch your system to video mode.'

I didn't need to ask the caller's name, or the reason for his call. Alex had warned me not to mess with this guy, but who cared? He was going to regret ever being born when I had finished with him.

'I'm coming for you, Venerio. If you've harmed my son, I will take you apart, piece by piece,' I told him.

'I have your pretty wife, or should say, *had* your bitch of a wife.'

'I have no wife; ask her.'

'Switch on and ask her yourself.'

I slammed the phone down and poured myself a large cognac, then switched my laptop to video mode and waited for the program to load, not knowing what to expect. The shock of seeing this woman who was my wife, with Venerio standing behind her chair, sent me reeling for more cognac.

'So, my slippery friend, if you have any love left for your *signora* or her *bambino*, you had better listen to me,' sneered Venerio.

His words hardly registered as I gazed in horror at the woman being forcibly restrained on a high-backed chair, in what appeared to be a Venetian palazzo.

'Save me.' Her harrowing cry cut through me like a spear, the sight of her long red hair knotted into the lattice work of the chair, unable even to raise her head, filled me with a murderous loathing for her captor.

As Venerio moved closer to the screen, his black leather jacket creaked, like some barbaric medieval jailer, reminiscent of the hood and beckoning hand in my nightmares.

'Tell Inez to bring every diamond in her possession to me here. She must come alone and unarmed, then she will sign legal papers transferring our fine family palazzo to me. For every day she delays, I will take her daughter, tame her, and put my bambino inside her.'

Giselle groaned like a wounded animal. 'Gaston, save me or kill me!' she screamed.

'And my son?'

'Your son is safe in the arms of Guido's daughter, for now.'

'So you would steal her inheritance? As Guido's daughter, she is the rightful owner of Palazzo Faconi, not you.'

'She will do as I say.'

'No, Venerio, I won't do as you say,' interjected a dark-haired woman as she came into view. 'You can have the diamonds *and* your ancient pile of rotting firewood. Give me a modern villa in the sun any day. As for Guido, he was no father to me; he left my mother to scratch the dirt for a living. I am glad he is dead, and congratulate the man who killed him.'

Venerio swung round to face the woman sitting quietly in the shadows, cradling my son. He walked towards her shouting and gesticulating.

'This is the *signore* who killed your father! You should kill him; our family's honour demands it!' he shouted.

At this, Luc began screaming. The woman spat in Venerio's face, wrapped Luc's blanket tightly around him, and ran from the room. Venerio returned to the screen, his face contorted in anger.

'Enough of this farce. My friend, you have 48 hours. There must be no tricks if you want your *bambino* to reach his first birthday. Meanwhile, I will entertain your pretty *signora*.'

Distraught and angry at seeing my son as a captive, I finished the bottle of cognac then went to bed. But during the night my fragmented memory began subjecting me to an eerie picture show, with unconnected flashbacks flickering through my brain as I slept the sleep of a seething drunk.

At sunrise, I woke with a rapid heartbeat and a monumental hangover, struggled out of bed, and went in search of my new mobile and Alex's phone number. Events of the previous evening danced like flames of fire in my memory. My God, I dared not think what other degradations Venerio had visited on Giselle overnight.

'Alex, don't ask questions,' I said. 'Venerio has my son and has kidnapped and violated Giselle. The sick bastard has threatened to continue on a daily basis until he has those cursed diamonds. We only have 48 hours, so get your ass to Nice airport as we need to get her out of there fast. Be careful what you say to Inez. I'll ring you later, now get going.'

Chapter Eight

At the airport, I received an uncompromisingly explicit call from Alex.

'You're on your own, mate. If Venerio wants the diamonds, he must come to us, bringing Giselle and Luc with him. Hope he doesn't shoot the messenger.'

I rang off in disgust and called Inez, but there was no response to any of my calls. These and other potentially life-changing events had unfolded so rapidly, leaving me no time to formulate an effective plan. Now faced with a seemingly impossible lone mission, my spirits took a downward turn.

After a smooth flight to Venice, I caught a *vaporetto* into the heart of the city, where the incessant rain did nothing to improve my mood. Tourist groups with large umbrellas gathered en masse around the main attractions, with the Piazza San Marco almost impassable due to the sheer numbers of people crowding around the Basilica.

Threading a path through the busy walkways, I mused on my current feelings for Giselle and her callous disregard in abandoning both our marriage and, more importantly, our child. Why *did* she move on so quickly after my disappearance? Was her new love already there in her life, waiting for the right moment to declare his feelings? Questions, endless questions, but would there be answers when I saw her face and heard her explanation? Would I know if there were residues of our love buried deep in the crevices of her heart? And did I feel responsible for her present incarceration?

After a short consideration, I came to the damning conclusion that the answers to all of my questions were a resounding denial of her good character. I walked on, holding the image of Palazzo Faconi in my hand, my head spinning with lurid imaginings of Giselle at the mercy of Venerio and his associates. Would I save her? Yes. Did I love her spoiled self-pity and her inflated sense of entitlement? No.

My love, like my memory, had been dashed on the rocks at Antibes, but yet again it was me who had been sent to save her. This latest family drama, like all previous Roxberg dramas, was all about their wealth, not my alleged crime of pushing Guido Faconi to his death at Villefranche.

Walking on, my eyes searched the impressive palazzos along the Grand Canal for the semi-concealed entrance to the water-gate at Palazzo Faconi, easily recognisable by carved grotesques depicting fox heads entwined by serpents, high above the principal entrance door.

With so little time to prepare for my visit, I had not thought to arrange suitable accommodation, and no doubt every hotel in the city would be brimming with tourists looking to enjoy the last bank holiday before the Christmas season. I had to think. My son's life depended on my next move, so there was no margin for error.

Putting my prejudices aside, I decided to call Alex.

'Where are you?' he asked sharply.

'Standing opposite the Faconi residence, where else? Do you have a mobile number for the au-pair?'

'Her name is Aria, but don't mess with her. She looks passive enough, but looks can be deceptive. So what's your next move? Not going to execute a one-man raid on Venerio, I hope, because you won't succeed.'

'It wouldn't *be* a one-man raid if you had honoured your offer to help. Know something, Alex? You're just a joker hiding behind Inez's money, pretending to be a man of action – or, in your case, inaction. Now just give me the number.'

I logged Aria's number into my phone then went in search of a secluded restaurant. Dangerous planning invariably included the help of a little *haute cuisine* and a quantity of alcohol. In the past I had devised many an escapade, but never on an empty stomach.

Hidden away in a quiet backwater, far from the usual tourist haunts, I found a friendly, family-owned seafood restaurant. An impressive-looking waitress came over, smiled as she handed me the menu, and asked what I would like to drink. After giving my order, I asked if she knew of any accommodation available at short notice, suitable for a family of four, as a workable plan had begun to formulate in my weary brain.

'*Si, signore,* but it will be very, very expensive. My house is near here, but I will be staying with my lover this weekend. His wife is away visiting her sick mother,' she replied, arching her back as she smoothed her skirt in anticipation of the pleasures to come.

'You are very trusting, *signora.*'

'And you, *signore,* have an honest face. Three nights, that is all I can offer you, but first you must show me your passport, *and* I will only accept cash in advance,' she said, giving me the inquisitive look of a practised opportunist.

'I assume your party includes a wife and children. Do you have a wife, and perhaps little ones?' she enquired openly.

'My party consists of my ex-wife, our baby son, and his au pair, here for an impromptu few days' break.'

'Some party; sounds complicated.' She laughed. 'You will need another break to clear your head. I will keep your number in case next time you need more than a break.' She laughed again, and I thought how pleasant bachelor life would be once Venerio was dead and life returned to some semblance of normality.

'Thank you, your suggestion sounds inviting. Maybe next year at festival time. Book me in.'

'Your patience is admirable, *signore*. I must be losing my allure,' she remarked huffily.

She gave me her bank details, then passed my order for lobster salad with a side of French fries to a food waiter.

'You run a profitable business, *signora;* a woman after my own heart,' I murmured in quiet complimentary tones, when she returned with my order of a bottle of Frascati.

'You French men are so full of crap,' she whispered in my ear while peering into her phone, presumably to confirm receipt of the transfer I had sent just a few minutes earlier.

'*Eccellente*, we have a deal, *signore*.' She fished a set of keys from her apron pocket, complete with directions and a map, all clearly typed and laminated.

'I see you are organised and well prepared for repeat business,' I commented wryly, waving the laminated page in her direction.

She turned, shaking her head. 'So full of French crap,' she said quietly as she walked away.

The house, a narrow three-storey merchant's dwelling, was more than adequate, with a hall lined with storage cupboards on the ground floor, a salon and kitchen on the second, and three bedrooms with a shared bathroom above. All in need of re-decoration but thankfully very clean, this house would serve my purpose.

Now for some fireworks. With a clear head and dishonest intentions, I texted Aria.

Aria, it's Gaston, here in Venice, offering you a lifetime of sanctuary in a country of your choice. Please bring my son to this address tomorrow.

She replied almost immediately.

We will slip out before dawn. Our servants are sympathetic and will facilitate our escape.

My heart soared with joy after receiving her reply. When Luc was safe, I would rescue Giselle and give Venerio the beating he deserved. The next two days of strategic planning would be vital to the success of my mission, especially as the only weapons at my disposal consisted of an ancient Army knife and two fists.

First, I would need to enlist Arno's help. The dignified old man had an unassailable sense of morals, so no doubt he would find this business distasteful and be glad to see us leave.

At this point, a thought occurred to me. Did Luc have a passport? And if so, which parent was it ascribed to? These and other pressing issues clouded my thinking over the waiting hours.

Café Villande was due to open soon, and a text from Iona confirmed she and Flora had sanitised the restaurant and filled the outdoor flower baskets with new plants.

My intention of giving Venerio a sound beating, rather than ending his life, presented me with a myriad of problems. If we gave in to his demands, would he go quietly or reappear at some point to threaten my family and staff.

Newly mindful of avoiding more disasters, I texted Mama.

Dearest Mama,

I am alone in Venice, attempting to rescue Luc and Giselle from Venerio's tyranny. Would you be willing to accommodate Aria and Luc, while I resolve other urgent matters?

With gratitude, Gaston.

I took a long shower then went to bed, still trying to convince myself that Giselle was strong and would hold out. She had to hold out… what else was there?

Mama rang in the early hours. She had obviously taken time to consider my request, and from her tone, it didn't sound hopeful.

'Gaston, my dear, as you intend rescuing Giselle, why bring Aria here, too? What purpose will she serve? Surely Luc's mother is better placed to care for him?'

How typical; how predictable. Why did she always erect barriers and want to change everything to her way of thinking.

'Mama, if you don't want to help, just say so straight out. Venerio and I shared a video call prior to my departure. Mama, he is using Giselle in the vilest way, and she will need hospital care if she survives.'

'Then yes, Gaston, do your best. I will make Aria welcome here for a short time. Inez says she is very attached to the child. Do you have a watertight plan?'

'Yes, Mama, now let me sleep. Aria and Luc will be here around dawn.'

'Gaston, you are my only son, please be careful. I couldn't bear to lose you again.' She'd said it; she'd actually voiced her concern for me for the first time.

Later that night, as the city quietened, I fell into a deep sleep, until somewhere in my unconscious mind there came an urgent tapping on the front door. Leaping from the bed, I raced downstairs wearing only boxer shorts, my heart pounding in my throat.

On the doorstep, Aria stood with her back to me, looking around scanning the passageway from right to left, alert to any threat. As she turned, I caught my first glimpse of Luc, tucked into a sling, sleeping contentedly against her breasts.

I stood momentarily blocking the doorway, such was my surprise. No-one had mentioned her ethnicity. Like an idiot, I had wrongly assumed Guido Faconi's daughter to be entirely of Italian parentage.

She handed me her bag and Luc's sleeping basket, then waved me aside. As she passed to ascend the stairs, her fragrance infused the air with a potent mixture of sandalwood and myrrh.

I watched with blatant admiration as she tucked my son into his basket, kissed his head and stroked his plump cheeks, then turned her dark eyes – her father's eyes – to me.

'When do we leave for France?' she demanded curtly. 'We must travel over-land, as Luc has no passport. Venerio has gone; he set sail for Villefranche last night. He must be stopped. You must kill him before he kills you for murdering my father. There will be no peace while he lives. He is taking your wife to her mother, where he will exchange her for property and diamonds. He is a devil, like my father. They are all devils without honour; they deceive, and they care nothing for family loyalty. They have the audacity to call my mother a Moroccan whore, when in reality she is an educated woman teaching the English language at a madrassa for females in Fez. She is a modern woman, worthy of great respect.

'Of course, money is their god, and they are welcome to it, but I have this child. We are like mother and son; we can never be parted.'

I found her breathless outburst and look of militant defiance rather irritating under the circumstance. And why was everyone so convinced that it was me who pushed Guido Faconi to his death?

'Aria, my promise to protect *you*, as *you* have protected my son, remains inviolable. However, the fact remains that it was *you* who illegally abducted my son, taking him to another country and placing him in a life-threatening situation.

In my opinion, *you* are at ground zero where my trust is concerned, so cease demanding and start earning,' I told her.

'Now, for my peace of mind and Inez's reassurance, a thorough inspection of the palazzo will be necessary to establish the current situation. Please ring the servant Arno and tell him to unlock the water-gate at noon today, as I wish to speak to him.'

She gave me a haughty look and reached for her phone. '*Bestia,*' she whispered as she scrolled through her contacts.

'I don't speak your language, so I'll take that as a yes,' I said, knowing full well that the word meant 'beast'.

She rang Arno and arranged the meeting, speaking in a rapid dialect I found impossible to understand. Then she switched off her phone and stood assessing me though narrowed eyes.

'They called you a reckless fool; a selfish man who disregards his own wife, so I stole your son to save him from your influence. Behave with honour or you will never see him again. And now, I want to sleep without your wife's screams ringing in my ears.'

'Fine, but hear this. Neither you, nor my son, are going anywhere without me. I have arranged for you to stay with my parents while I resolve this situation, then you can decide to stay or leave – entirely your choice.'

'I will not leave Luc. You have no idea how to care for him; he needs my protection.'

She tucked Luc into his basket then disappeared upstairs to rest. Of course, she was right. Having had no experience of children, and less so of babies, I decided to step back and let her call the shots – that is, until we reached France.

After checking the front door lock, I made coffee, then lay on the sofa to muse over Aria's comment about 'Giselle's screams'. Thoughts of her suffering at the hands of Venerio and his cronies filled me with seething rage. Again, Aria was right. Venerio had to die for us all to move on.

Somewhere in this complex city a bell chimed 5am – time to wake Alex the joker. The news of Venerio's departure should be enough to wipe the smile off his smug face. Now it was his turn to feel the heat.

'Not dead yet?' answered Alex.

'No, my friend, your turn next. Aria tells me Venerio has set sail for Villefranche. He intends to exchange what's left of Giselle for Inez's diamonds and signed transfer documents with regard to the ownership of Palazzo Faconi.'

A sharp intake of breath could be heard at the other end of the line. 'I will find Inez and video call you.'

'Call me this evening. You need to hear this from Aria herself.'

'Not sure Inez will agree to speak with her. Aria is beyond *persona non grata*. Just remember, Aria entered our household under false pretences and stole Inez's precious grandchild,' remarked Alex curtly.

'If Inez had cared for my son, she would not have needed an au-pair. And seriously, Venerio left her with no choice: take my son or lose her life. The guy is terminally deranged.'

'Leave it with me. Maybe she can be persuaded, although it's doubtful.'

Well, that piece of news has wafted a breeze up that joker's kilt, I thought. *Serves him right for refusing to help me.*

Feeling restless, I left the house to breathe sea air and plan my next move. I had taken the precaution of locking the front door, in case Aria had second thoughts and decided to remain in Italy. An hour later, armed with sweet breakfast cakes and fresh orange juice,

I returned and ran upstairs hoping to find Aria in a more cooperative mood.

The welcome aroma of freshly brewed coffee greeted me. Aria had found eggs, butter, and milk in the fridge, and was busy coaxing Luc with tiny spoonfuls of scrambled egg. She had showered and changed into a white dress, her long black hair, oiled and dripping from the shower, had left damp patches down the front of her dress. My heart lurched at the sight of her. I was lost in awe at the sight of this exotic Madonna feeding my son.

'Look, Luc, your papa runs like a child and stinks like a camel.' Her confident, self-assurance were qualities I had never seen in Giselle.

'Ok, I get the message,' I replied.

'When you are cleansed and fed, we must plan our escape,' said Aria, pointing to the shower.

'No doubt you have suggestions.' My voice was lost in the sound of running water.

'Oh yes, leave it to me.' she said, walking into the bathroom and handing me a towel. To my amusement, she stood openly assessing my physique.

'You are too full around the waist; your heart will suffer when you are old,' she remarked, eyeing me critically.

'Hopefully you will stay around to keep me on track.'

She rolled her eyes and shrugged. 'Nice try, but don't flirt. Men flirt all the time. It's meaningless.'

'I'll keep that thought in mind when choosing your wedding ring. As for safety, we will be travelling as man and wife.'

'Gaston, it is possible for a man to be clever and stupid; unfortunately you are both. So, if you think a ring will allow you access into my bed, think again. I am 32 years old and have yet to be touched by any man. Only my true and legal husband will enjoy that privilege.'

What's this, a 360 degree *volte-face?* Now she was talking marriage. That's what I would call rapid progress.

'Aria, you have my word that I will respect your legendary virginal status until we reach home waters. Thereafter, it will receive my full attention.'

She frowned and waved her hand dismissively.

'Your approach is indelicate, *mon cheri,*' she said softly, her voice rippling like a drowsy stream.

'My apologies, *signora.* I will await your instructions with breathless anticipation.' She sighed as if she had heard my pathetic attempt at verbal foreplay a thousand times. Nevertheless, I like a woman who holds out on me. This one was quite unlike any woman of my acquaintance. She had the sinuous strength of a lynx and the resilience of my mama!

'Now stop this nonsense, we need to plan. Do you have money, as we need to buy a car large enough to sleep in?' she enquired with an air of no-nonsense practicality.

'Yes, yes, we can do that later, after I have seen Arno.' With my patience on a knife-edge, I gathered up my son and took a deep breath.

Aria had it all worked out, and we planned our escape route over coffee and toast. First, Verona on to Genoa, then to the safety of my parents' home at Antibes, where I would leave Luc and Aria until Alex and I had rescued Giselle and disposed of Venerio.

We agreed Aria would drive to Verona, as she was more familiar with the route than myself. Thereafter,

I would complete the journey, which she estimated would take around 24 hours, including comfort breaks. Once again, strangers like Aria, Venerio, and Alex were interfering in my life, and while I accepted that their involvement was necessary, my recognition of them as individuals remained a mystery to me. Maybe rehab had not been so bad after all.

Luc gurgled away as he drank orange juice from a spouted cup, his eyes never leaving my face – eyes that in shape and colour were identical to my own. His hand in my hand formed an unbreakable bond between us.

Aria came over and ruffled his abundant dark curls while gently squeezing my shoulders.

'Gaston, I feel your stress. This is understandable, as you have suffered, but for Luc's sake we must stay strong. Your escape from the boat left Venerio with no choice. You forced him to change his plans. He believes you killed my father, so you were the target, not Giselle. *She* would not have been abducted if *you* had not escaped.'

'Oh, so it's my fault? Why am I always the fall guy? Please allow me to remind you that my name is Villande, not Roxberg, and definitely not Faconi. So right now, I regret meeting every last one of you. Now, I must leave, Arno is expecting me.'

Aria's calm reasoning had done nothing to restore my mood. The last thing I needed was her damming explanation of why my ex-wife was in mortal danger.

'Must you go? Arno will have made the necessary arrangements. You may be shocked to hear what he has to say,' said Aria impatiently.

'What is there to arrange, and why are you trying to prevent me from talking to him?'

She sighed resignedly. 'There may evidence of Giselle's ill treatment. Evidence that Arno will want you to witness. Should Giselle decide to prosecute Vanerio and expose us all to scrutiny, the authorities will examine every line of enquiry. We would all be under threat of incarceration if she makes a complaint. Do you want that? Do you want Luc to discover his papa is a murderer?'

She had a point, but what she didn't know was that Giselle would never betray me, of that I was sure.

'All the more reason to meet him and insist on his silence,' I replied. 'Lock the door behind me and don't let anyone enter.'

She placed her hand on mine. 'Please believe me, I did try to stop him many times, but it was useless. He is a very strong man… Look, unzip my dress.' She turned around. 'Go on look, see for yourself.'

Reluctantly, I unzipped her dress, revealing her bruised back, laced with red wheals where she had been beaten. Silently, I closed the zip, then took her in my arms and kissed her hair. In return, she took my hand – her gesture of acceptance, her acknowledgment of my impulsive need to comfort her, the perfumed warmth of her burnished flesh pressing into me, coaxing me to comply with her wishes.

'He must be stopped,' she said, looking directly into my eyes. 'Together, you and Alex must stop him. There will be no peace until he dies.'

Ok, so her assessment of the situation was correct. Venerio would be put out of action permanently, and I intended to do just that.

'Aria, thank you for trying to save Giselle and for protecting Luc.'

She lifted her face and kissed my mouth, a luxuriously generous kiss which ignited every fibre in my body. Then she abruptly stepped away in embarrassment, apologising for her brazen behaviour.

I wondered afterwards if she was playing a game to ensnare me with a covert invitation to either initiate her first intimate experience or the promise of further intimacies to ensure my compliance. I bolted for the door in uncharacteristic fashion, never usually being one to run in the opposite direction from a beautiful woman.

On route to the palazzo, Alex rang to say Inez had refused to speak to me or Aria, but had taken herself off to the bank, in a state of extreme agitation, to retrieve a small quantity of her precious diamonds.

'If she imagines Venerio will be satisfied with a few stones, she is deluding herself,' I told him. 'What's the plan? Are you intending to tackle him yourself, or hide behind the authorities? Either way, leave me out of it for now. My immediate concern is bringing Luc and Aria home to Antibes.'

'Why Antibes?' questioned Alex.

'I want to distance them from the potential danger zone until we have neutralised Venerio.'

'We?' questioned Alex again.

'Yes, we. You're not having all the fun. And anyway, I need to square things with Inez. Like or not, she is Aria's stepmother and Luc's grandmother.'

'Trust me, that counts for nothing where Inez is concerned. She will never trust Aria again, and neither should you. You seem quite protective of her. Is there anything you care to share?'

'Too soon. If she is hiding anything, it won't get past me. The most annoying problem is Luc's lack of a passport, which will necessitate us traveling over-land to avoid any over-zealous border control checks.'

'No problem, mate, I have already sent an old friend to collect you. He will ring tonight to arrange a rendezvous. Aria will recognise him as the guy who has been inviting her out for romantic dinner dates these past six months. The poor guy is besotted.'

I ignored his reference to Aria's personal life.

'Oh right, so you do have your uses, after all? Thanks, I owe you one. I'm off now to speak with Arno, to hear his version of events and check the palazzo for vermin like Venerio.'

I walked purposefully along the Grand Canal, admiring the splendid palazzi lining its route around the city, and found Arno standing forlornly at the private water-gate to the palazzo. Dressed in his usual attire of a black tailcoat, resembling a displaced penguin, he brightened and drew himself up as I walked towards him. He had aged noticeably since our previous meeting just six or seven months ago.

'*Buongiorno, Signore* Gaston, welcome to our sad palazzo,' he said wearily. 'My wife and daughter are still away. I thank the Holy Mother they were not here to witness the sins perpetrated by Venerio on Aria and that unfortunate young *signora* Giselle. I am an old man, unused to such violent behaviour. I cannot bring myself to wash away the evidence of the young *signora*'s shame, as the authorities will need to see the evidence of Vanerio's crimes. *Signora* Inez will want to prosecute him; this is a very serious matter.' His distress was evident as he rambled on, regardless of my protestations.

'Thank you, Arno. We will not be involving the authorities, and I will have to insist on your absolute discretion in this matter. The family will deal with Venerio. He will never trouble you again.'

He stood aside for me to enter the grand hall, where past generations of the Faconi family had celebrated happier times. The large, shaded room held a dark all-pervading air of menace. The once opulent red velvet curtains hung in shreds from their elaborate pelmets, shrouding the intense southern light; intricately carved ebony furniture had been stacked without care at the far end of the room; and the once impressive minstrels' gallery had gaps in the balustrade.

Arno looked away, unable to meet my look of appalled astonishment at the damage caused by Venerio and his associates.

'*Signore* Venerio and his guests have ruined our beautiful entrance hall. We are ashamed. What will *Signora* Inez think if she sees this careless damage to her property?' The poor man looked downcast and wholly defeated.

The stench of sex and alcohol hung in the air like clouds of impending evil. Looking around, I waited for my eyes to become accustomed to the deeply upsetting scene before me. On a semi-circular performance stage, situated under high, stained-glass windows, sat the chair on which Giselle had been tethered by her hair. Now it was knotted with strands of her long red-gold tresses, left hanging as a stark reminder of her pain and degradation, while on the floor tiles underneath the chair were streams of blood and ejaculate – more damning evidence of her torture.

'This was Venerio's doing,' I exclaimed, turning to Arno.

'Yes.' He nodded sadly. 'And others.' He averted his eyes. 'My shame in being unable to help her will stay with me forever. I am an old man and my strength has faded,' he said dejectedly.

I felt sickened and enraged. How could any sane man subject a woman to such unimaginable horrors? This was too much for me; she was my wife, my friend, the mother of my son. I vowed there and then to find her and give Venerio the death he deserved.

Bracing myself, I took images of the scene, while Arno stood behind me trembling with fear and shock at the atrocities he had been forced to remember.

'Poor lady, we heard her suffering and could do nothing to help her. He would have killed us if we had tried to interfere.'

'We both need a drink. Do you have any cognac in the house?' I turned and placed a steadying hand on his shrunken shoulder.

'In the cellar, *signore*,' he said, pointing to a door near a lift serving the upper floors.

'Is there a light switch? Cellars make me shudder.'

'*Si, signore*, next to the lift switch.'

Minutes later, we sat sipping cognac to steady our nerves.

'Arno, are you and your family happy to stay here, after all that has happened? Or would you rather live quietly in the country, away from this crowded city?'

He shook his head. 'Venice has been my home since boyhood; I was born here and will die here in this palazzo. Signora Inez has promised us a lifetime without fear of eviction, so we will stay. Please come back to us with love in your heart. Bring your family, your friends, bring us your joy and laughter, like the old days when *Signore* Guido's parents were alive.'

A flush of heat stained my face at hearing Guido Faconi's name – the man I had pushed to his death off the harbour wall at Villefranche. I promised to return just to please the old man, but knew the promise would never be kept.

'Arno, can you shake my hand with honour and promise me Venerio is not hiding here in this building? My time is short. Too short to be searching this place.'

He offered me his hand. 'Be assured, *Signore* Venerio and his friends have gone and they have taken the poor *Signora* Giselle. They set sail yesterday. May the Holy Mother save her,' he said, a wan smile creasing his weary face.

'Thank you for your assurances. Now I must go. My regards to your family, and please remember, you are highly valued by us all.'

After leaving the palazzo, I walked around aimlessly for about an hour, desperately trying to quell the urge to leave Venice that day. Wild imaginings of the suffering and degradation Venerio had inflicted on Giselle burned like glowing embers in my memory. He would not be allowed to live, that was for sure.

The bright sun of late August had finally dissolved the remaining threads of mist shrouding the Basilica and campaniles. My wanderings led me back to the quiet backwater and to the restaurant where, two days earlier, the friendly waitress had agreed to rent me her home at an exorbitant price. A waiter caught my eye and came forward to take my order, and was immediately brushed aside by my hostess.

'*Buona sera, signore*, my house is to your liking? Perhaps you wish to stay longer?' she smiled and raised her perfect eyebrows.

'Yes, I do like your house. However, we will be leaving tomorrow morning, as agreed.'

She seemed disappointed at losing so lucrative a client.

'The house belongs to my lover.' She gave me a confidential wink. 'I make money when he is absent. Winter is approaching, a time when tourist revenues become scarce, and tips are few. Are you ready to order?'

She took my order of two seafood platters: one boxed and chilled for Aria; the other for me to enjoy with a large glass of vino to steady my nerves. I wondered if my food preferences were embedded in my wavering memory, or merely a random choice from the menu. There would be time enough to seek expert advice in the coming months.

While waiting for lunch, I rang Alex. He answered my third call.

'How's things?' he enquired urgently. 'Inez is frantic to hear good news.'

'Actually, it's worse than I thought. No point in attempting to disguise the fact that Giselle has been used abominably by Venerio, and possibly his associates. My gut reaction tells me she won't survive the journey after the abuse she's been forced to suffer. And if she does, her life will change irrevocably. So don't give Inez false hope, because currently there is none.'

'Ok, this is my take on the situation. We will go on the offensive and launch an operation, rather than sit and wait for Venerio to arrive at Villefranche. Giselle needs to be taken out within the next two days, so your main priority is to leave Venice tomorrow, as planned. When Luc is safe with your parents, you will be required to provide back-up. I will arrange your transport.

'Incidentally, your in-bound car transport has reached Verona and will be in touch later. Don't ask his name, just ring me before boarding,' said Alex convincingly. 'And one more thing... presumably Aria will have Venerio's mobile number. We need it to get a fix on his position.'

'Joker turned ex-army commander, what other surprises do you have in mind?'

'Gaston, wise up and get real. Giselle's life is hanging on a thread. This is serious. She is Luc's mother, don't you feel any compassion for her?'

'Initially yes, after hearing Arno's account of her ill treatment. However, I have no recollection of the woman who divorced me in my absence and abandoned my son. There was no explanation of her feelings, no contrition, and not one letter of intent from her lawyer awaiting my return; she simply moved on regardless. Quite honestly, she means very little to me.'

Occasionally harsh words ring true, expressed by people like me who have everything to lose. Selfish attitudes are a life-preserving mechanism for people who value the safety of their family above all else. Since meeting Luc, I had become a devotee of this line of thinking; serious thoughts which had necessitated a change of plan. As Alex would soon discover, there would be no back-up, no dangerous escapades, and definitely no murders... although maybe a few corrective beatings might be required, if Vanerio persisted on his current trajectory.

Back at the house, I found Aria and Luc asleep, enfolded like puppies in a basket. Her phone lay on the side table, together with items of prepared baby food. Obviously she had ignored my advice to stay indoors.

Quickly scrolling through her contacts, I found Venerio's number forwarded it to Alex, then deleted the contact as a precautionary measure. The only person I trusted right now was myself.

The aroma of hot coffee woke Aria and she surveyed me anxiously, looking for signs of anger or disgust.

'You saw Arno?' she questioned, lowering her eyes.

'Yes.' I gave her a long searching look.

'You know what happened in that house of hell. No point in discussing it further.' She looked relieved and slightly furtive.

'So, you ignored my advice to stay indoors,' I remarked wryly, indicating to the newly purchased baby food and biscuits on the table.

'There is a rear door; the key was there left in the lock. You are too trusting. Venerio may know this and use it to his advantage. And, Gaston, please remember I am a free spirit. My kind do not take instruction; we live by our own rules.'

'Well, Aria, hopefully your free spirit will enjoy this seafood platter from the restaurant,' I replied teasingly.

'Ah, so it's fine for you to eat in restaurants, while I am locked indoors caring for your son,' she huffed.

'After a few months in my restaurant kitchen, you will have had enough of them,' I told her. 'Now go and eat. We have a long journey ahead of us.'

Glancing at my phone, I saw a text from Alex, advising us to meet our driver outside the train station at eight this evening. He gave a description of the vehicle and the registration number.

We had five long hours to wait, prior to our rendezvous, so I suggested that Aria continued to top-up on her sleep reserves, as she would take the first drive to Verona. My suggestion, though, was met with derision. As my current mood was anything other than conversational, I decided to take myself off to bed.

Four hours later, Aria roused me with a sound shaking.

'Wake up, Gaston, it's nearly time to leave,' she hissed in my ear. 'Luc has been fed and changed. He will sleep until morning.' Her light musical voice sounded full of excitement.

Pausing momentarily, I asked her a straight question. 'You're not sad to be leaving? Italy is your home. You may inherit the palazzo in time.'

She shrugged. 'That palace of evil is not my home. There is no sadness in my heart, only elation at my release from Faconi domination. My heart remains in Fez with my mother, but for now, I will be the girl from Fez living in France with you and Luc. Now hurry, you must prepare. We have an adventure before us.' Her infectious enthusiasm for the long journey ahead began to lighten my own more anxious mood. Like Aria, I longed to reach the safety of home, to hear Iona's scathing comments and Flora's gentle teasing. But of Giselle there was nothing; no memory of her face or of our lives together. Her photographs were all that remained of our ten-year marriage.

I headed for the shower in an effort to dispel my fears. Vague thoughts of Flora, and of how she would receive our headstrong au-pair, floated through my head. Aria could occupy Giselle's old suite of rooms and become an integral part of the household. There must be no friction between us if we were to maintain a viable business. But first, we had to concentrate on reaching Antibes without arousing suspicion.

If questioned, I feared that Luc's non-existent identity documents might lead the authorities to believe he had been stolen to order.

Chapter Nine

We found our driver – a muscular, clean-cut military type – standing by a capacious vehicle, doors open ready to leave. He called us over, his eyes fixed firmly on Aria. She exhaled and whispered 'not him' under her breath, then turned her back to him. He stepped forward, offering her a steadying hand and took Luc, sleeping soundly in his basket.

'You're in the back,' she said curtly. 'I will drive to Genoa, then Gaston will take over for the remainder of the journey.'

'Come on, Aria, I have driven for hours just to see your lovely face,' he said, looking offended.

'Get in the back and go to sleep,' she repeated firmly, then turned to me. 'Gaston, I have driven this route many times, so please relax and try to sleep. We can stop at Verona if necessary.'

No argument, I bowed to her greater knowledge, settled into the front passenger seat, and closed my eyes to think and plan.

When Venerio came looking for me, he would begin his search at my home, not the home of my parents. And by my estimation, his journey would take considerably longer than ours, depending on his route. It was time now for Alex to step up and take his share of the crap.

As we journeyed on, pleasant thoughts of hearing laughter and cooperation in my restaurant kitchen, and excessive amounts of carnal pleasure in my bed, might soon be realised if my luck held. Parking my concerns, I texted Iona to say the restaurant opening would be further delayed until the end of September, due to unforeseen circumstances. Then I rang Alex to ask if his plans had altered.

'Where are you?' he barked into the phone.

'On route to Verona. Do you have a fix on Venerio? If so, what's the plan?'

'Aria got it wrong, or tried to put us off the scent. The *Volpe* is still at her moorings in Venice. Venerio is traveling the same route as you. It's obvious, as Aria is well aware, that only an idiot would travel such a distance by sea. It could take weeks and Aria knows that. She is a Faconi; don't trust her.'

Aria heard his remark and raised her eyebrows.

'I don't trust anyone, least of all you,' I retorted sharply.

'You have to trust me. I know too much,' Alex replied sourly.

Of course this was true – for the time being. But later, when this mess was over, Alex Forbes would need to re-calibrate his life… or I would do it for him.

At the outset of our journey, Aria and I had agreed to keep any conversation between us to a minimum, as Luc needed his sleep and the inquisitive driver had been supplied by the opposing camp. This, though, this did nothing to satisfy my curiosity as to her past. In my experience, long car journeys usually provided a perfect opportunity to gently prise information from my captive traveller.

I glanced in her direction. Her face was a silhouette of concentration on the road ahead. Soon it would be my turn to drive, then she would discover my ineptitude at the wheel.

Around midnight, the tall towers of Verona loomed out of the darkness, casting their long shadows, as we drove slowly through the darkened city, hoping to find a late-night café. Luc stirred in his basket and opened his eyes. He smiled and raised his plump arms in recognition as I reached to cuddle him.

'There is a service station with an all-night café about ten kilometres from here. I need to top up my caffeine levels, and a tiny someone needs a nappy change, judging by the atmosphere in here,' said Aria, opening the window slightly to allow much needed ventilation.

At the service station, we abandoned our comatose driver, still slumped on the rear seat, and went in search of coffee. The place looked well used but the coffee smelled good. The guy serving behind the bar smiled as we entered and reached for the television remote to lower the volume.

'*Buona sera,*' he called, shaking his head and gesturing towards the screen.

'A beautiful, young *signorina* found floating like a gondola. So tragic. Such a waste,' he said, shaking his head despairingly.

Aria and I turned our stricken faces to the screen in dread of what we were about to see or hear.

'Where?' My heart began to pace, sending blood pounding through my ears.

'In a venetian lagoon,' he said pitifully, shaking his head in disbelief. 'She had been drinking. These accidents happen; boats and alcohol can be a dangerous cocktail. What can I get you?' he asked, changing the subject.

Aria and I stood like wax figures, transfixed to the spot by the impending horror unfolding before us.

'Has she been identified?' I asked, holding my breath.

The barman shook his head. 'No, *signore*, she was found wearing nothing but a flimsy nightdress. No-one knows who she is.'

I passed Luc to Aria, her face paled with shock, her downcast eyes brimming with unshed tears.

'Gaston, please, don't ring Venerio,' she pleaded. 'He will discover our whereabouts, then we will all suffer.'

Her words were lost in my mountainous anger: anger at Venerio; anger at myself for my delay in rescuing her. We were too late. We should have, could have, done more. Now my life would be overshadowed by her death.

I went out outside, scrolled through my contact list, and pressed the call button beside the letter V. He answered on the second ring.

'Shut your mouth and listen. I'm coming for you. You're already dead.' I pressed the end call button.

Two minutes later, he texted.

'Your beautiful ex-wife chose to dive overboard and swim with the fishes. Her choice: stay with me, swim to safety, or die.'

I returned to the café, my mind imploding with rage. Like me, Giselle had attempted to escape Faconi aggression via water. Thoughts of her struggle and shuddering surrender took me back to the swirling iridescent waters and treacherous rocks off Antibes, to the hood and beckoning hand seen there and later in my nightmares. Was this my path to death? A path taken willingly ten years ago on my marriage to Giselle Roxberg?

Mama's prior knowledge of the Roxberg family, together with her warning of the emotional turmoil to come, had gone unheeded in the throes of passion.

With my courage at its lowest point, I rang Alex.

'What's wrong?'

There were tones of concern in his voice, but it was obvious he had not yet heard of the body found floating in the lagoon.

'Bad news; in fact, dire news. Giselle jumped ship, or was pushed. The body of a female was found floating in the lagoon earlier today. If my fears are confirmed, you will have to break the news to Inez, then fly with her to Venice to identify the body and organise Giselle's repatriation.'

There was a long silence at the other end of the line.

'Did you hear me, Alex? There is a distinct possibility that Giselle is dead.'

'I heard you, and yes, it is her. Venerio tried to prevent her, but she resisted, saying she would rather die than bear his child.' His voice broke with emotion.

'That was not the plan; she was not meant to die. We just wanted the diamonds the family owes us. No-one was supposed to die.'

A few moments flickered past before the runaway train of what he had just admitted hit me.

'*We?* What do you mean *we?* Are you telling me that you and Venerio planned this whole diabolical charade in order to steal Inez's diamonds? I will turn you murdering cretins over to the authorities – that is, after beating the crap out of you.'

'No chance, mate. Not while I have a video of you pushing Guido Faconi to his death off the harbour at Villefranche. Giselle's death was a tragic mistake; your crime was premedicated. So don't get clever with me, or we will silence you, permanently.'

'Ok, so tell me one thing, does Aria know any of this? Is the woman feeding my son in a roadside café complicit in murder?'

'Not ours, mate. As I said, it was never our plan to kill anyone. It's true Venerio had a thing for Giselle, but that was just sex, not murder.'

'Oh yeah, that bastard killed her the moment he laid his filthy hands on her. I saw the evidence of her ill treatment. He won't get away, and neither will you when Inez hears the truth. Or do you intend to kill her, too?' My question hung in the air momentarily.

'No-one needs to die if they keep their mouths shut and follow orders. If you try to stop us, you and your entire family will suffer for your actions. And if the authorities are informed, we will all be spending the rest of our lives behind bars. So cool it,' said Alex calmly.

'I had bad feelings about you from the start. So how did you meet Venerio?'

'Henry Roxberg and Venerio's cousin Guido needed help with the shipments of goods from Italy to Roxberg Gate. Their fake pictures and furniture provided us with a lucrative family business, all kept well under the radar.'

'You're not family; you're nothing!' I spat the words into the phone.

'You *know* nothing. Henry Roxberg was my biological father. Typically, he refused to marry my mother, but eventually he agreed to pay for my upbringing and education.' He hesitated before continuing. 'One freezing winter's day, I found my beautiful mother lying face down in the woods at Roxberg Gate, her mouth stained with poison berries. The verdict was suicide, but we all knew that evil bitch of a housekeeper, Margot du Val, was responsible. She poisoned every woman who came near Henry.

'His refusal to explain why he allowed her to continue only intensified my dislike of him, so I left and never looked back... until we heard about the diamonds. Ask Iona. She knows everything—'

I cut him off mid-sentence. This was the final blow. How many raw emotions could one man endure in the space of 24 hours, and now Iona, my friend and trusted employee, had withheld information vital to our safety. His words stuck in my throat like bile. All involvement with these tainted Roxbergs needed to end before I lost my mind.

The cool night air sharpened my senses as I walked back to the car. The driver was still comatose on the rear seat, a bottle of sleeping pills in his hands. This guy was Alex's accomplice so he would be the first to go, I decided. With a degree of satisfaction, I grabbed his ankles and slowly levered him out of the car. The guy must have overdosed, as he was still asleep in the forecourt shrubbery as we drove away into the night.

As the smoky pink dawn rose over Genoa, Aria and I were almost incoherent through lack of sleep. With our driver ejected, we had been free to spend the night openly discussing our thoughts regarding the dangers currently testing our strengths and frailties; every last one of them had been laid bare, honest and unadorned by insincerity or guile. But would I want to continue my association with a woman whose family had caused the death of my son's mother?

The busy port city of Genoa lay quiet and virtually traffic-free at that hour. We made our way across the sprawling city, heading out towards the coast road and the French border. At that point my energy levels were definitely running on empty. We all needed to eat, sleep, then formulate a plan, although two members of our party were oblivious to my fatigue. I looked enviously in the rear-view mirror at Aria, curled under a blanket on the back seat, with Luc asleep in his basket, tucked safely in the rear footwell.

As we left the city behind, the seemingly insurmountable obstacle of Luc's passport had yet to be resolved. If we attempted to book into a hotel, the desk attendant would expect to see his name included on my passport, but this might be less likely in rural accommodation, such as a farmhouse gite. Pulling over at the next layby, I searched the web for somewhere nearby to rest for 24 hours.

Aria emerged from under her blanket, bleary-eyed, asking why we had stopped when her planned rest break was just ten kilometres distant.

Note to self: I must learn not underestimate this female.

'My dear Aria, I have many vainglorious qualities, however mind-reading is not included in my extensive repertoire.' We both laughed as I stumbled over such a pompous pronouncement of my attributes.

'When we are married, you will be allowed access to everything,' she smiled confidently.

'Can I take that as a proposal?'

'Of course. Did you not understand?' Her sultry accent deepened when she was teased.

'That's agreed then,' I said, thinking the exact opposite while transferring my signet ring to the third finger of her left hand. 'Now, please drive me to food and rest.'

Aria changed Luc's revolting nappy, then jumped into the driving seat and checked the sat-nav directions on my phone, while I attempted to sleep through a chorus of noisy squeals and gurgles from Luc.

We arrived at the farmhouse – a low, stone building, well hidden in a wooded valley roughly one kilometre from the nearest main road – as the family were all sitting down to breakfast. The aroma of smoked ham, eggs, and coffee sent my tastebuds into a state of ecstasy.

Aria explained our situation to the owners – a friendly couple with young children of their own. They offered us breakfast and a spare room in the attic, as their tourist accommodation was fully booked. The children played with Luc while we feasted on local ham, mushrooms, and eggs taken from the coop that morning. My caffeine habit would have to wait until later, as my need for sleep was more important.

Aria handed me a large glass of orange juice and pushed me towards the stairs.

'Now sleep. We still have some distance to travel.'

I fell onto the nearest bed and allowed oblivion to claim me. Waking at sunset to find Aria sleeping soundly in the bed opposite gave me the opportunity of studying the soft contours of her face and the swell of her breasts. Groaning with the effects of unspent passion, I made a quick dash to the nearest bathroom to relieve myself, then padded downstairs to find Luc lying on the floor, thrashing a toy trumpet. As he caught sight of me, he kicked his legs excitedly and held his arms out to be cuddled. Our hosts had packed a light supper of panini and fruit to eat on the journey home.

I noted their address, paid the bill, and left an enormous tip, promising to return next spring. With my strength revived, I was ready for anything. A plan had been formulated, now all I had to do was execute it.

Chapter Ten

As we drove away and onwards into the balmy autumnal night, a feeling of sublime contentment washed over me. With Aria at the wheel, wearing a determined expression, and Luc sleeping soundly in the rear footwell, I felt a sense of family connection for the first and only time since leaving rehab. When we grew closer to the French border, an urgent call from Alex ended my burgeoning feelings of contentment.

'Change of plan, mate. Inez and I are leaving for Venice within the hour. My decision to stay with her and see this out means you will have to deal with Venerio. If he hears of me double-crossing him, he will be adding my name to his hit list. But I am not prepared to leave Inez now; not after losing Giselle. She is consumed by grief and beyond inconsolable. Giselle's death changes everything.

Now, listen up, you need to get your parents away to safety. Venerio is heading for Antibes, and he will exact his revenge on anyone connected to your family. He is determined to avenge Guido. And don't forget you started this, so you can finish it. So here's the deal: you keep your mouth shut about my mission, and the video will be deleted.'

I half-listened to his proposal through a vortex of panic.

'Deal, now get off the line.'

If that double-crossing joker thought he could call the shots, he could think again. Frantically, I rang mama..

'Mama, don't speak, just listen. You and Papa are in great danger. Venerio Faconi is on his way to you. He holds me responsible for Guido's death and intends to take his revenge on anyone connected to me. He abducted Giselle and kept her prisoner, but sadly she died as a result of his ill treatment. In essence, he wants Inez's wealth and me dead. I will meet you at Jules' restaurant at San Remo. Now go.'

'Gaston, you are a living nightmare, but we will do as you ask.' A click, and she was gone.

There was no answer from Jules' mobile phone, so I rang the restaurant thinking he was busy serving customers. To my surprise, Flora answered the phone.

'Hello, Flora, have you deserted me for Jules?'

She laughed. 'Hi Gaston. No, of course not. Your restaurant is closed and I was feeling lonely, Jules rang to check on my welfare and said he needed a front of house. He pays more than you and his staff don't bite. Where are you?' Her voice held an unmistakable note of tension.

'On my way to you with Luc and Aria. So are my parents. Now, Flora, listen carefully. It's imperative you find Jules and ask him to arrange hotel accommodation for us as soon as possible. We will need three rooms for an indefinite period.'

'Why? What's wrong? What have you done now? Not another of your escapades, I hope.'

'Flora, please just do as I say.'

Aria looked at me and rolled her eyes.

Seeing San Remo again would inevitably evoke memories of my long stay in rehab, but the advantage of staying close to the border would facilitate our entry into France unnoticed, via the Alps Maritime. We drove on through the night with Aria at the wheel, her face a picture of steely determination.

'Do all babies sleep like the proverbial dead?' I asked.

'Only the well cosseted ones. Play your cards right and that could be you eventually,' replied Aria with a smile.

Yes, she had a point. But moving my life forward to a more peaceful phase remained an, as yet, unrealised ambition.

Just then Jules video called, asking for the latest developments and offering his home as a refuge for us all. His welcome gesture was quite unexpected and took me by surprise. In the past we had enjoyed the occasional dinner at either of our restaurants, but our families had never socialised until now. I suspected he was harbouring a secret motive.

'So, my friend, what are your plans for Flora? And don't give me any nonsense about needing a front of house. You have enough front for ten restaurants.'

'She admires my personal magnetism, and what's more, I have fallen deeply in love with her.'

I found his declaration of love amusing.

'If Flora is a representation of your mid-life crisis, you have chosen well. Not sure Iona will agree, unless you direct a large portion of your personal magnetism in her direction.'

'Ah, not so. Both she and her strange partner dined here with us only last week. I have their blessing and am just waiting for the right moment to propose. No chance yet, though, with the escalation of your latest drama.'

Feeling slightly disturbed by Flora's rapid ascendancy in Jules' affections, I wondered if the basis of her affection was of the material, and therefore insincere, type rather than borne out of genuine feeling. After all, she had recently declared her undying love for me. Jules and I were both in our late thirties, so perhaps Flora was subconsciously seeking a father figure, especially as her own father was long dead.

After three hours, I woke and took the wheel, while Aria fed and changed an increasingly restless Luc.

'He wants to play; he is tired of being trapped in his basket.' She transferred his basket to the front footwell where he played with his favourite toy rabbit.

'Talk to him, she urged. 'He will begin to recognise your voice.'

Luc gurgled and kicked his plump legs while I spoke, eyeing me occasionally with infantile suspicion, his attention focusing mainly on his toy. Aria sighed with exhausted relief, then lay on the rear seat and pulled a blanket over her bare legs. To my astonishment, she fell sound asleep within minutes of us resuming our journey.

Her satin smooth hair fell across her face like a waterfall of ink, the swell of her breasts straining at the creased linen shift she had worn for the past two days. sending waves of sensual expectation coursing through my blood. I wanted to see her naked. Naked and pregnant with my child, her nipples oozing with milk to feed our new-born life, but these and other desires could never be voiced. Too risky in these days of enlightened female empowerment.

In an effort to stay alert at the wheel, I began to evaluate my thoughts regarding the threat of male emasculation in the worlds of education, politics, and commerce, by women determined to attain and maintain positions of power and influence. Women like my mama who, within marriage, had found it necessary to sacrifice family obligations in order to boost the family's finances and further their careers. Whereas now, we red-blooded Frenchmen were constantly discouraged from voicing our carnal thoughts and sexual predilections due to absurd, over-zealous political correctness. Even my own countrymen, known throughout the world for their obsession with the female form, were severely castigated for any unguarded remarks or lecherous glances when a beautiful women or man entered our lives. It's nature; why fight it?

I shouldn't compare. Mama said comparisons were odious. No-one is ordinary; we are all exceptional in our own way. Aria possessed the qualities so lacking in Mama, and in appearance a stark contrast to the images Inez had shown me of Giselle. Now, sadly, after my life-threatening encounter with Venerio, my memory of her had been further erased. Giselle was the mother Luc would never know; the mother who abandoned him at birth for his close resemblance to me. If Venerio thought he could deprive me of my life and my son, he could think again. He had already taken too much. It was my turn to deprive him… of his life.

As we grew closer to the French border, my longing to seek solace in my beloved Menton became harder to resist. In my mind I could smell the French air, the perfumes of Grasse, the lavender in Provence, and the aromatic coffee in Nice's historic quarter. After much deliberation, I allowed my reservations about leaving Aria and Luc alone and unprotected at Café Villande, to overcome my selfish inclination to head home. Any deviation from our plan would be too dangerous to contemplate, knowing Venerio's intentions.

When we reached the outskirts of San Remo, Alex attempted a video call. I cut him off then returned his call.

'No pictures, Alex. What do you want?'

'Where are you?' he called affably.

'None of your business. Where is Venerio?' I snapped.

'Take it easy. Just looking after your welfare,' exclaimed Alex.

'Just lately, your care has been careless. Now where is Venerio?'

'He has arrived in Antibes, so I hope your parents are not at home.'

'How long do you and Inez intend to stay in Venice?' I questioned.

'The authorities won't release Giselle's body until after the post mortem, so we will have to stay until after Giselle's cremation. And don't think about gate-crashing the funeral, Inez said she would rather die than breathe the same air as you. Incidentally, your driver was not impressed at being dumped in a wayside bush and left for dead.'

'Then he should have treated Aria with the respect she deserves. Now listen to me. If you fail to delete the Villefranche video, Inez will definitely see me again, and she won't like what she hears about you being Henry's son.' I cut his reply mid-sentence and drove on.

The late summer sun had burned away all traces of lingering sea-mist, leaving the sky a sublime Mediterranean blue. Aria woke suddenly, looked around, and asked me to find somewhere to stop for a comfort break. I leaned over and squeezed her arm reassuringly.

'Five minutes to our destination, then you can have all the comfort you need.'

She smiled, leaned forward, and touched my hand.

'I just want you… and Luc,' she replied warmly.

Chapter Eleven

The sat-nav guided us directly to Jules' spacious villa on the outskirts of the city, and my heart sank as we entered the tree-lined drive. There on the front lawn, seated at a long table shaded by an ancient cedar tree, we saw Flora, Jules, and my parents enjoying a very early breakfast. Flora's stray terrier 'Thing', now seemingly a confident member of the household, was busy nibbling every crumb that came his way. A sharp intake of breath from Aria alerted me to her feeling of apprehension.

'Don't worry, you will be made welcome here.'

'I am a Faconi. They will dislike me and try to send me away,' she remarked nervously.

'Aria, you are wearing my ring. Trust me, they will say nothing to hurt you.'

She gave me a dubious look but remained silent.

As we came to a halt, Jules and Flora hurried over to greet us, while Mama and Papa focused their attention on Aria and Luc, who had woken and begun to demand his breakfast.

'Thank God you're all safe. Your rooms are ready, but join us for breakfast when you've freshened up,' said Jules, giving me a hug. Without hesitation, he tickled Luc's nose and kissed Aria's hand.

'Welcome, Aria. We might wait all day for Gaston to introduce us. Never seen anyone look more exhausted.'

'Thanks, Jules. Give us half an hour to shower and attend to Luc, then if you don't mind, we need to sleep.'

'Not at all. You must excuse me as I have a business meeting at the restaurant, but we can talk over dinner this evening. Flora will show you around, so if you want anything, just ask her.'

With that, he sauntered off to his convertible, then drove off waving and sending sprays of gravel in all directions.

Mama and Papa called and waved. As we walked towards them, I noticed their hands linked under the table like illicit lovers, and wondered what had happened to bring about this miraculous reconciliation. Papa stood awkwardly, holding on to the table for support. Had he suffered an event during my absence?

'Mama, Papa, may I introduce my fiancée, Aria Faconi, and my son Luc.' A few moments of shocked silence was broken by Luc demanding his breakfast in the strongest terms.

Mama responded coolly to my announcement, while Papa limped around the table to give Aria and Luc a polite hug. 'Welcome to our family, *cherie*. Later, when you have rested, we must all talk and get to know each other.' Here came the dreaded inquisition I had hoped to avoid.

'Fine, so what happened to your leg?' I asked, changing the subject.

'Fell down the stairs in my bookshop. Lay there for two days with a broken leg before a customer found me,' he said with a cheeky wink.

'Two days and only one customer? Time to sell the shop and concentrate on staying alive,' I remarked with a smirk.

'Yes, Gaston, and after your latest misadventure has ended, I suggest you do likewise.'

Chastened but undeterred, I ignored his comment. My parents must never hear the whole truth of what happened at Villefranche on that fateful day when Guido Faconi lost his life through my impulsive action, or of my present intention to silence Venerio. Of all my concerns, Alex's video of the event was the most pressing. He had has shown himself to be secretive and untrustworthy and his influence over Inez appeared to be unassailable. Although, when she hears of his blood connection to Henry, she would be forced to make a difficult choice: accept him as the man she loved; or terminate their affair and his employment, then be left with nothing. Two daughters and two husbands, all dead.

'Gaston, Flora is calling.' Aria roused me from my reverie with a soft caress of her finger on my cheek. Sensing my unease, she squeezed my hand.

'Come on, you two, your rooms are ready,' called Flora from the terrace. 'No specific allocation, so you can choose whichever you like.'

As we entered the house, Flora attempted to take Luc from Aria but was resolutely rebuffed.

'Luc will need time to accept strangers,' said Aria, stepping out of reach. 'We are like mother and son; we are inseparable.'

'How will he grow accustomed to his family if you keep him to yourself? He is too young to decide who will care for him,' remarked Flora airily. She turned her back on Aria then slipped her arm through mine.

'Gaston, tell your au-pair not to concern herself. From now on, I will care for Luc. Go on, tell her.'

She turned and faced Aria. 'You are not needed here. Perhaps you should leave and go back to your home. Italy is where you belong.' Aria took a step towards her, her face a study of icy disdain.

'I have betrayed my family for this child and his father and my life is in danger. This is not a game, so please accept that we are all staying until it is safe to leave,' said Aria softly, so as not to alarm Luc.

Aria's calm assertiveness in the face of Flora's open hostility was fascinating to watch. She appeared undaunted by this houseful of strangers, some of whom had valid reasons to doubt her sincerity, even though now was not the time for them to express their doubts.

'Flora, please remember your manners. Jules has offered us a place of refuge, as Aria has already explained. We need to stay here for a few days. Time enough for you to reflect on your rudeness.'

'Fine,' she said sharply, 'but tell me this, I couldn't help overhearing part of your conversation with your parents. Correct me, but did I hear something about a marriage?' she said, giving me a long, speculative look.

'Yes, Flora, you heard correctly. Aria has accepted my proposal.'

'But what about *us*?' she shouted angrily.

Aria tactfully excused herself by saying she had left something in the car. I turned back to Flora, my patience hanging by a thread.

'Flora, there is no *us*. You are like a daughter to me; someone to educate and nurture, nothing more.'

'You lied to me. You led me to believe we would be together when your problems were sorted, and now, after so short an acquaintance, it's all about you and the woman who stole your son.' Her face contorted with tearful anger. 'Gaston, she is a Faconi, she can not be trusted!' shouted Flora, her anger rising to a crescendo. 'You *must* remember, everything was agreed with Giselle's blessing, she entrusted Luc to my care. I read countless childcare books, organised the installation of his nursery and the clothes he would wear. You allowed me to believe in our future. You are cruel and callous!' she cried vehemently, her eyes brimming with tears.

I laughed. I couldn't help it; she looked like a toddler in a tantrum. Ok, so maybe I did allow her to hope there might be a chance for us, but thankfully, I'd had the sense to resist her recent advances. She was too young. I knew it then, and her behaviour today had confirmed just that.

'Flora, you know I am still suffering from amnesia, so how could I possibly remember your agreement with Giselle? Our situations have changed. Luc needs Aria. She has cared for him since birth and he loves her. It would be cruel to separate them. She will become Luc's legal stepmother, so please dry your tears and stop behaving like a spoilt child. Aria and I are well matched; we live by our own rules. You are kind and sweet.'

'And boring,' she interjected hotly.

'It wouldn't have worked; you are too young. We enjoyed a father-daughter relationship, not husband and wife. Now, let's start again – that is, after you've apologised to Aria. Dry your tears before anyone notices.'

Flora accepted my explanation with a grudging reluctance. She was young and would love again.

My thoughts returned to Jules and to our conversation regarding his, as yet, unspoken feelings for Flora. In her present mood she was likely to refuse him, and as a valued friend, his happiness was important to me. So, if I was the only impediment to their happiness, I must leave – and soon.

Flora dried her tears then led me up two flights of stairs to the top floor. Both of our interconnecting bedrooms overlooked the lush, well tended gardens, and beyond to the sea. When I went to the window and looked out, my heart filled with pleasure at the sight of Luc sitting astride Papa's knee and Aria in deep conversation with Mama. *Is this my new beginning?* I wondered. *Is this where and with whom my destiny lies?*

'Well, Gaston, if you don't love me, I shall stay with Jules. You can make a new daughter with your new wife,' said Flora cuttingly, then left the room in a huff and ran downstairs. 'I'm driving into town,' she called up from the hall. 'The fridge is full. You can make your own meals, but Jules wants us all to have dinner here, so I will see you later... if you're still here.'

I watched from the window as she walked over to Aria and Mama, held a brief conversation, then sped away down the drive out of sight. I headed for a shower, wondering if Flora had offered Aria an apology. Arguments could wait; what I needed now was to sleep.

Around 4am the following morning, Aria woke me – phone in hand – saying Arno was asking to speak to me. My body flooded with adrenaline as she handed me her phone. This could only mean one thing: trouble.

'*Signore* Gaston, it's happening again. *Signores* Venerio and Alex are here and they have locked *Signora* Inez in her room. I overheard them shouting, telling her she must consent to marry *Signore* Venerio. She is weeping, lamenting for her dead daughter. My wife cannot bear to hear her grief.' Arno's voice cracked with emotion.

'*Signore*, we cannot live under threat. I am an old man, my heart is weak, and my wife is dying of heartbreak and disease. In two days, these infidels will be dead then we will have peace. You must return to Venice, and together we will dispose of their bodies,' he said with absolute finality.

'Arno, don't be foolish,' I warned him. 'You're incapable of overcoming two strong men half your age. Now listen, if you want my help, you must delay your plan for another 24 hours. I'll ring you before boarding the plane.'

'I am no fool, *signore*, there are many ways to kill a man. I will leave it to nature. Nature will kill them, then together we will throw their corpses into the canal.'

Call it self-preservation or just honest selfishness in agreeing to help him, knowing that if we were caught, the blame would be his and not mine. It would be very convenient for me, as Alex's death would release me from the constant threat of disclosure or blackmail. He had lied to keep me in France, out of reach until after they succeeded in marrying Inez to Venerio. As her husband, he would be legally entitled to get his filthy hands on her wealth, including the Roxberg diamonds.

'Arno, go to bed and rest. I promise to be with you within 24 hours '

Aria had sat quietly, listening to our conversation. I threw her an accusatory look, my eyes questioning her sincerity. Would *she* betray me for a share in the Roxberg wealth?

Gauging my expression, she waived her religious principles, offered up a whispered prayer to the Holy Mother, asking for fertility and forgiveness, then slipped into bed beside me. We came together in reverend union. She surrendered her purity, her sacred gift, as proof of her fidelity. And I was a man lost, drowning in the magnificence of this woman. Her intriguing aura of mystery excited my senses and satisfied my passions – a goddess personified, and she was mine. Finally, we slept until Luc woke us, demanding our full attention to his needs.

'Before we part, there is something I must confess.' There was a sadness in her eyes, and for a moment I feared she might reject me.

'I fell in love with your son, but I am afraid to love you, for now we must live for Luc, for his safety, his future. When your business in Venice is concluded, we must content ourselves with family and friends, rebuild our lives without sorrow or regret.'

'Easy for me. I have no regrets or a previous life to remember. So, you don't love me?' I gave her a quizzical look of mock sorrow. 'You love my son, but not me?' This was a massive ego blow, so I wouldn't push it.

'It will take time to learn to love a murderer,' remarked Aria seriously.

She was correct on every level. The back catalogue to my life regularly alternated between abysmal tragedy and serial comic instances of bad luck, saved only by my self-depreciation and bloody-mindedness. Only a brave optimist would consider taking me on. But she was my only route back to a normal life, and I needed to take it.

We all picnicked sprawled out on blankets under the ancient cedar. Papa spent the afternoon entertaining Luc, while Mama and Aria swam then ensconced themselves in the orangery, with the door firmly closed. Putting thoughts of Venice to the furthest corner of my mind, I decided to ring Iona.

'Oh, ye still alive then? Still have no manners to speak of. We could be dead for all ye care. *And* Flora tells me ye are in deep trouble again, and of all disgraces ye are marrying the au-pair.'

'Stop, Iona, I don't need or accept your ill-informed censorship. Where are you?'

'Staying with my cousin in Northumberland, if it's any of your business,' she replied testily.

'Good, I suggest you stay there and seek employment, as you will not be returning to Café Villande. You are dismissed.' This time, like many previous times, she had gone too far.

'Ye can't do that, we're a family, the Roxberg outcasts. Ye can't mean it,' exclaimed Iona.

It was amazing how people with an overbearingly forthright manner always assume they have the right to judge everyone but themselves.

'What if I apologise?' she wheedled.

'No point. You can have three months salary as a parting gift... Goodbye.'

In the words of some prophet or other, life changes. And although Iona and Flora were extremely close confidantes, as close as mother and daughter, that didn't excuse their rudeness. Iona's ill-concealed disapproval of Aria would have surfaced at some point, causing recriminations and feelings of discontent. Now more than ever, I wanted a marriage of equals, based on unconditional love. But for now, our pipe-dream future depended entirely on my forthcoming mission to Venice.

As the afternoon heat intensified, I went for a cooling swim then joined Papa and Luc, who were both drowsing in the shade.

'You and Mama appear to have settled your differences. I saw you holding hands under the table earlier.' I gave him a boyish nudge.

'Yes, my fall bought us to our senses. Of course, she insisted I sell the bookshop and meet my female friends in public, but these are small concessions to make for a peaceful life.' He sat up and gave me a purposeful look.

'When are you and Aria thinking of getting married? None of my business, of course, but I hope you're not marrying her because of Luc.'

I understood his concern, but at the same time felt irritated by his comment. If Mama shared his concerns, perhaps we should keep our distance for a while and take Luc to visit Aria's mother in Fez.

Just then, our peace was shattered by the sound of spraying gravel, announcing the arrival of Jules and Flora. She waved and walked over carrying two large bags of food.

'Hello, everyone. We came armed with ingredients for a traditional Moroccan feast. Now we need to persuade the expert to prepare it – that is, if she knows how to cook.'

Flora's barbed comment did nothing to impress Papa, who gave her a look of undisguised disgust. Jules, blinded by the mirage of infatuation, looked on in sublime ignorance.

I stalked off into the house to find Aria, and found her asleep in my bed. Not wanting to disturb her, I crept out and went for swim in the shallow end of the pool to cool my temper. Later, Aria appeared looking refreshed and very inviting. Her journey into sexual awakening had imbued her with a noticeable radiance, and simply being together in the same room gave me an uncontrollable urge to take her upstairs.

Flora perched herself on a kitchen stool and asked who was cooking dinner, as she had had her nails painted bright red and was definitely not going anywhere near a paring knife. I thought how much she had changed since my return from rehab. Gone were her long, tawny curls and fresh, scrubbed face; her natural look had been replaced by blonde-streaked hair and voluminous make-up, which detracted rather enhanced her looks. Since beginning her affair with Jules, she has acquired a superficial veneer of sophistication, unsuited to one so young and with minimal life experience.

Her attitude to Aria had turned my pseudo parental affection to disappointment-tinged relief, as she would lead a safe and comfortable life with Jules.

She watched closely as Aria spoon-fed Luc at the kitchen table, her eyes narrowed like the arrow slits at Roxberg Gate.

'Aria, will you cook dinner for us this evening? We have bought the ingredients and would love to try the cuisine of your *native* country,' said Flora silkily.

Her blatant emphasis on the word 'native' irritated me beyond words. I wanted to cause a scene, but somehow managed to keep my rising temper in check.

'I will be your sous chef,' she continued smoothly. 'So if there is a disaster, I can take over and change the menu.'

Aria looked up from feeding Luc and smiled serenely.

'Fine, you can start by peeling two artichokes, then de-stone 30 grams of cherries, please,' said Aria pleasantly, ignoring Flora's offensive comment and returning her attention to Luc's noisy demands for more food.

'Sorry, have new nails. Perhaps Gaston would oblige? In the past, I have found him very obliging,' said Flora sneeringly.

Just then, Mama and Papa entered the kitchen carrying blankets and trays littered with empty cups and twice-read newspapers. They were just in time, as a rumble of thunder could be heard in the distance which, together with Flora's barbed comments, had spoiled the tranquillity of our afternoon. Soon after, a short deluge of thundery rain cooled the air and raised the humidity.

'Papa and I are going up to shower and change, then I will help Aria cook dinner,' announced Mama firmly, while giving Flora her well practised look of disapproval. 'Flora, you can arrange the flowers, Gaston will be sommelier, Papa can play with Luc, and Jules – our generous host– can amuse us with anecdotes from his early life.'

Turning to me, she placed her hand on my arm.

'Gaston, your papa and I will be leaving for Antibes tomorrow, and Aria and Luc will come, too. When your dreadful business in Venice is concluded, I want you all to stay with us. We have matters to discuss, and a wedding to arrange.'

'I think you may need help in Venice,' interjected Jules. 'Arno is too old to cope with Alex and Venerio alone. I will come along for the ride, to keep you company or dig you out of a hole.'

'Thanks, but no, this is my fight. Don't get involved. It's going to be violent and very bloody, and I would never forgive myself if you were injured.'

'What's the plan? Come on, don't keep us in suspense,' urged Flora.

'Let's drop the subject and enjoy our last evening together,' came my reply.

'You make it sound like the Last Supper. And if you get caught, it will be,' said Flora, as she flounced off into the garden to gather flowers.

We agreed to meet in the dining room at 7pm, then went our separate ways.

I lay on the bedroom sofa and slept until the alarm woke me at 6pm, having booked my return flight to Venice for the following day. In the dining room, Flora had arranged a centrepiece of scented flowers from the garden, and laid the table. Candle flames, dancing in the early evening dusk, injected beams of light into an assortment of crystal glasses. Vague memories of similar occasions filtered through my mind, and any subliminal feelings of isolation might have been lessened if only I could have remembered when those occasions had occurred.

Jules appeared carrying two bottles of champagne, a beaming smile creasing his sunburnt face.

'Let me guess. You proposed, and she accepted.'

'Yes... It's strange. I always thought she preferred you, but at times women can be very secretive,' he replied. 'So, two forthcoming marriages to celebrate tonight, although I would imagine you're in no mood for anything until Alex and Venerio have been dealt with. I dread to think what Inez has been forced to endure. Have you heard from Arno and how he intends to murder them?'

'He texted earlier. The inner door of the water gate will be left unlocked, and he expects me tomorrow evening around 8pm. 'Nature will kill them,' that is all he said. Enough for now; I hear footsteps.'

Jules had guessed my mood, and yes, it was anything but celebratory, so I would resort to alcohol for a little help.

Everyone looked so amazingly elegant under the circumstances, as none of them had packed evening wear for their short stay, except Flora, who dazzled in a revealing, gold strapless cocktail dress. We all drank two glasses of champagne in rapid succession, and Jules drooled like a love-struck teenager at the sight of Flora in her finery.

When Mama appeared, carrying the first course of Aria's aromatic feast, we turned our full attention to the serious business of food. Papa delivered the second course served on a silver salver, upon which sat three poussins, stuffed with cherries, herbs, and spiced bread, followed by dishes of fruited rice, artichoke couscous layered with anchovies and capers, and a mountainous tabbouleh salad. Aria wore Mama's elderly black chiffon dress – a garment I had seen many times, but never so elegantly worn.

I was a little drunk but didn't care. After tomorrow, my problems would disappear. No more Roxberg or Faconi dramas. I wanted to feel a cool metal band on the third finger of my left hand and a bed warmed by my new wife.

'No third course, we must respect our waistlines. Especially you, Gaston,' said Aria in all seriousness.

Mama dissolved into giggles as all eyes turned to my torso.

'As a traditional Frenchman, I live for making love and fine cuisine,' I replied. 'Lately, the severe shortage of the former has encouraged my indulgence in the latter.' Everyone fell about laughing in response to my mock-pompous lifestyle preferences.

We ate, drank, and laughed to excess, and as the evening lengthened, we spilled out onto the terrace to sip cognacs and drink black coffee. We sat stargazing as the still, humid air of late August hung over us like damp lace. Daytime butterflies were replaced by enormous, brightly-marked moths, irresistibly drawn to our citrus-scented candles.

Strangely, the subject of my forthcoming mission to Venice had been avoided all evening. At 11 o clock, Aria wished us goodnight, taking Luc along with her. A feeling of longing came over me as I watched her disappear into the house.

Mama noticed my look and smiled.

'Well, Gaston, this time you have made a wise choice. Aria is kind, resourceful, and level-headed, rather like myself, and quite unlike Giselle, with whom I never felt the bond of kinship.'

'That will do, Vivienne, we should not speak ill of the dead. She was, after all, Luc's mother, and I thank her for giving us a grandchild. God willing, we may have many more,' said Papa giving me a wink.

'Look, you old rogue, will you take Mama to bed? Jules and I have important matters to discuss.' They departed soon after.

'Jules, my friend, if it all goes wrong tomorrow, will you see to it that Aria and Luc are safe? I have written a makeshift will and would ask you to witness it.'

'Yes, of course. Actually, I was going to ask if I might rent Café Villande for a year. My idea of expanding the business appeals to Flora and would give you time to rebuild your antique business. Gaston, it might be necessary for you to leave the country for a while, depending on the outcome of events in Venice.'

'Yes. Actually, I am planning to visit Aria's mama in Fez, but haven't mentioned that to her just yet. Everything depends on Arno's plan to eliminate Alex and Venerio, and I'm not afraid to admit to feelings of mortal terror, knowing what they are both capable of. Arno will need to be one brave genius to outwit them.'

We said goodnight. Upstairs, I looked in on Aria and Luc, sound asleep in their room, then went alone with my fears to bed.

Chapter Twelve

At dawn, Aria slipped between my lavender-scented sheets, and we came together with feverish abandonment, like parting lovers in wartime, not knowing if we would ever meet again in our lifetimes.

'Gaston, you are twice the man they claim to be, but be warned. I have a greater knowledge of both Alex and Venerio, and they will not think twice about killing you or anyone who stands in their way. Listen to Arno and follow his instructions to the letter. You must avoid capture, but if you are unsuccessful and the authorities are informed, go to my mother in Fez. Luc and I will meet you there.' Aria spoke like a general mustering her troops.

'Understood. Now come here.'

We sank into each other's arms for the last time, then slept until Luc's demand for attention woke us. Startled and hungry, we rushed into Aria's room to find Luc out of his basket, rolling around the floor. He looked up and raised his arms to be cuddled, his plump face wreathed in smiles of pleasure at his latest achievement.

'I feel as though he is really starting to acknowledge me,' I said, tickling his tummy and throwing him in the air.

'It takes time to bond; don't rush him,' remarked Aria, while meticulously packing their few belongings into a canvas bag in readiness for their stay with my parents at Antibes.

Later, we all gathered for breakfast on the terrace. Our mood, like the weather, had a subdued expectancy. The threatened storm of last evening had failed to materialise, and the air, heavy with the scent of jasmine and roses, held an intoxicating stillness. Amongst us, there was a distinct sense of foreboding. Today, our lives would change; today, I would become complicit in two murders and, if Alex and Inez were truthful, wholly responsible for the death of Guido Faconi.

I stood watching as my family disappeared down the drive and out of sight, my palpable sense of loss reinforced by the stark realisation of the danger I must face in order to protect them.

Just then, Flora appeared from the side kitchen door, carrying a basket for collecting flowers to decorate the hall. No doubt she had seen Aria drive away with Luc and my parents.

'Oh, they've gone. Good. Jules will be leaving shortly, then we can talk sensibly about us.' She slipped her arm through mine, pulling me towards her in a way I found acutely embarrassing.

She knows there is no us, so why does she persist? I wondered. If Aria had not entered my life, then maybe, in time I might have accepted her, together with that period in my life that had gone.

'Gaston, please don't speak, just hear me out. It's hard for me to accept that after all we have been through together, you still fail to reciprocate my feelings for you. I waited for you, those long months not knowing if you were alive or dead. I am heartbroken; you have stolen my happiness. Aria is an au-pair, and she cares for your child, so understandably you feel indebted to her. But, Gaston, you are confusing love with gratitude. Please allow me to demonstrate the depths of my love for you. Your flight is hours away, so come to my room after Jules has gone.'

I turned to face her.

'Flora, it's quite simple. I don't love you. Never have. And what about Jules? He would be devastated if he heard of your deception.'

'You won't tell him.' She stepped closer, her face flaming in temper. 'If you say anything to Jules, you won't live to regret it.'

Her ridiculous threat was completely out of character and not worth taking a shot at. I pulled a clownish sad face, and she retaliated by slapping my face so forcefully I could hear bells ringing in my ears.

'That's settled then,' I called after her, as she stomped off down a brick path leading to the flower garden.

'Don't speak to me,' she wailed, then she disappeared from sight.

Speak? I was too stunned to speak, and very upset for Jules. He had no idea that the teenage girl he intended to marry was attempting to pull his best friend.

I needed to leave; I needed to have a back-up plan should anything go wrong. I turned and ran back to the villa, said goodbye to Jules, then phoned for a taxi to the airport.

While waiting for my flight, I rang Arno to confirm our arrangements.

'Nothing has changed, *signore*, the lady is still locked in her room. They have called a priest – the same infidel who married her to Vanerio's dead cousin, Guido. He will perform the ceremony here tomorrow night, so we must kill these murdering infidels tonight and dispose of their bodies before more lives are destroyed, including my own and my wife,' said Arno self-righteously.

'Arno, how do you intend to kill these two strong infidels?'

'*Signore*, I have already told you, nature will kill them,' he retorted impatiently. 'Now, most important, please listen, *signore*. There is a service entrance to this beautiful palazzo at the end of our side canal – a plank of wood serves as a bridge. I will leave the door open at six o'clock. Stay away from the main city routes, as you can trust no-one. Vanerio's spies live in every corner of our magnificent city. Goodbye, *Signore* Gaston.' A click, and he was gone.

Obviously, Arno failed to consider himself a murdering infidel. His amusingly random concept of double-standards appeared inapplicable to him personally or to his wife. However, his devotion and loyalty to Venice and the Faconi name would be wasted then lost when Inez died. After this evening, she would have only one living full-blood relative – my son.

When my flight was announced, the stomach-churning reality of my mission hit me like a two-ton truck. Just then, Aria video called to reassure me they had reached Antibes safely, and of my parents' delight at having their only grandson and prospective daughter-in-law safe under their roof.

'Gaston, please keep your involvement in this sordid business to a minimum. Let Arno execute his plan, then leave immediately,' she urged. 'I will stay awake waiting for your call, in readiness to assist in your escape. I love you.'

'We all love you!' they chorused.

Arriving in Venice, I looked around with a heightened awareness, as strangers do when entering a foreign country. Now I was faced with the inevitable ordeal of negotiating Departures, in the hope of emerging unscathed from the many tourists crowding the hall, all vying to queue for Passport Control and a quick exit.

My phone read 4.30 – time enough to grab a coffee fortified with a double cognac, while reading a newly purchased street map. Avoiding the usual tourist trail would be a new experience, as I had rarely toured the lesser-known routes around the city, used almost exclusively by Venetian residents.

If Arno was to be believed, my contribution to tonight's drama would be minimal, so a little alcohol would ease my anxiety. Leaving the comparative safety of the airport gave me an unnerving sense of vulnerability, as if everyone around me had paused their lives, just waiting for my next move. These and other irrational fears persisted as I walked towards a public water taxi, and my instinct to run back to the airport was overwhelming.

As I turned, Alex's driver friend – the guy I had unceremoniously dumped in a bush and left for dead on route to Genoa – put what felt like a gun to my stomach.

'Don't make any sudden moves or you're dead,' he growled.

Instinctively, I kneed him hard in the groin, then ran to the nearest departing water bus. Other passengers looked on with mild interest, then returned to taking scenic photos.

A well of rage rose inside me as I paced the deck. *Just wait till I catch up with Arno, the shrivelled, double-crossing little rat*, I fumed.

Someone was shouting, 'Hey! Hey you!' And I turned to see Alex and Venerio watching me from the deck of an adjacent vessel.

I was trapped by my own fear of deep water and their determination to capture me. As their vessel came alongside, they quickly disembarked and stood waiting at the exit. I bolted to the nearest restaurant, hoping to find a rear exit through which to escape. But they had anticipated my move, and instead of making a clean getaway, I ran straight into Venerio, who resembled a reimagined black-bearded pirate and stank like a drain.

'So, my friend, we meet again. I will enjoy our last hours together, as this time tomorrow you will be dead,' he sneered.

The back door opened and in came Alex and his driver friend, who walked over and punched me full in the face. The blow sent me reeling to the ground.

'There's more of that later. I'm going to enjoy paying you back for running out on me,' he said menacingly.

'He's almost cold out. Let's kill him here and get it over. We have more important business ahead. I came here for money, not murder,' said Alex urgently.

Venerio rounded on him. 'This imbecile caused the death of my cousin Guido, and you think he deserves a quick death? No, my friend, I will see him suffer, then I will kill him myself,' said Venerio savagely.

Alex reluctantly nodded his agreement.

'We are all armed,' he told me, 'so no heroics. Get up and face the wall.' He frisked me then clipped two dog leads to my belt, handing one to the driver.

'Let's all go for a walk. Nice and calm; we don't want to frighten the tourists,' said Venerio smiling, his black eyes glinting with spite.

'So, tell me who squeaked,' I managed.

Alex gave me a scornful glance. 'A woman scorned is an unpredictable beast.'

'Flora!'

'Yeah, mate, your sweet Flora, who might have become my sweet wife, but no, you introduced her to Jules. Yes, she betrayed you, you heartless user. Well, this is payback time, and you richly deserve what's coming to you.'

Stunned and angry, I walked slowly with measured steps, my face beginning to swell. Fear and dread of the pain to come filled me with despair. The carefree voices of people jostling us along our route began to recede, like echoes of a passing procession. One moment, it was all banners and noise, the next silent awe at the spectacle they had just witnessed.

Arriving at the palazzo, we found Arno standing at the open water-gate, his weathered brow creased in concern. His tiny, bird-like eyes hardened as they rested on my bleeding lips.

He bowed to Venerio.

'Master, the *signora* has been calling for you, she wants her freedom. She has not eaten for three days, and my wife says she will sicken and die before she becomes your wife.' As Arno lowered his head, a ghost of a smile passed his lips.

'She will eat with us tonight, and watch as her husband's murderer is punished for his crimes,' Venerio replied.

A shadow of menace crossed the old man's face. 'She will not eat with you or sit at your table. Her daughter is dead; she is in mourning.' Arno's voice held a quiver of uncertainty.

'She will be made to watch his punishment and witness his death,' roared Venerio angrily.

They dragged me into the great hall, where Venerio took my phone and ordered me to remove my shoes. Then he chained me to the very same chair where he had repeatedly violated Giselle.

'Your pretty wife sat on this ancient chair – a Faconi relic, used by our noble family for religious ceremonies. I worshiped her on it many times,' he sniggered.

I spat in his face, and his eyes narrowed as he returned my gesture of loathing contempt.

'She was nothing!' he shouted, his face flamed with alcohol. 'Pale and spineless as a waning moon, of no use to any man, that's why she jumped overboard. She was a coward, but tonight we will judge your strength, my friend. Then we shall see if Aria's choice of husband is worthy of our noble family name.'

He walked towards me, grinning like some medieval torturer, then stood on my bare feet. I screamed out a string of expletives as he ground the heels of his boot into my bare toes.

'My friend, you need lessons in bravery.' He pushed my head back with his fist

before disappearing upstairs.

I sat fighting tears of pain and blinding anger. There was no escape; I was doomed to die here in this house of demons. Hopefully, my death would come swiftly and without prolonged pain.

My anguished thoughts returned to Aria, to my son and parents. Should Venerio decide to visit his wrath on them after my death, who would protect them? He was capable of exterminating our whole family, and all because I had the misfortune to fall in love with Giselle Roxberg. So this was how it would end – in pain and regret. *I should not have come here*, I admitted to myself. *I should have lured my enemies to French soil, then fought them on my own terms.*

As the afternoon lengthened, my feet began to numb and bruise, the feeling reminding me of the hypothermic episode I had suffered after my near-death experience on the rocks at Antibes. My head felt light, as if floating above the chair on which my captors had chained me. Looking down, I saw myself lying there unconscious and wondered if this was what death felt like.

Suddenly, a firm grip on my shoulder brought reality spiralling back.

'*Signore* Gaston, wake up,' whispered Arno's wife, as she shook me awake.

'Drink this quickly now, before the master sees.' She spoke urgently while standing over me, her skeletal frame concealed beneath an ankle-length, black dress. A glass containing a large cognac quivered in her weathered hand.

Ribbons of pain crossed my eyes as I raised my head, opened my mouth, and swallowed most of the strong alcohol laced with honey. It stung then soothed my blooded lips, and as the burnished liquid seeped into my veins, a warm, reviving feeling literally raised my spirits.

'They have taken my phone,' I told her. 'Please, will you ring Aria? Tell her what has happened.'

She tutted and waved her arms impatiently. '*Signore*, you think I have time to talk? Ring her yourself when your ordeal is over,' she replied testily.

'What do you mean "all over"? They intend to kill me tonight.'

'*Signore*, please listen. My husband has already told you; we have a plan.'

'Then please execute your plan before Venerio executes me,' I replied urgently.

'*Signore*, we have lived in the evil shadows cast by this family of devils, and waited a lifetime to take our revenge. No-one will be allowed to spoil our pleasure at seeing them writhe in agony. You must wait. Have patience, *signore*. Patience is said to be a virtue... even in France.'

She gave me two pills and poured the remaining cognac down my throat. 'Swallow, and you will feel nothing,' she ordered. Then, clutching her walking stick, she turned and ambled unsteadily from the room.

She wasn't exaggerating. Within minutes, my whole body surrendered to the alchemy of alcohol and her dubious pills, their hallucinating effect rendering me lifeless. I descended from pain and terror into a hazy, soporific stupor, incapable of coherent speech or rational thought. These weird sensations remained, while figures floated back and forth across the room, no doubt making preparations for a meal to celebrate my imminent death.

At some point, a bucket of ice cubes cascaded over my head, and I looked up sharply in an attempt to focus on my assailant. The room, now in semi-darkness, smelled fragrantly toxic. As my eyes became accustomed to the gloom, I could make out the figures of three men and a woman, all sitting at a long table covered in white linen, on which silver cutlery had been laid for several courses. The men were drinking wine as if it were cordial, calling vile slurs to Inez, while she sat quietly in the candlelight, secured to a chair with fine strips of leather, her head lowered in defeat. Watching her there, abandoned and alone, imbued me with burning rage against these inhuman defilers of decency.

As the melting ice sank into my clothes and down over my blood-soaked feet, reality began take hold.

'Nice trip?' bawled Venerio. He was so drunk he could hardly stand.

Alex and his driver friend laughed into their wine glasses. Inez shifted uncomfortably in her chair then glanced over and mouthed 'sorry'.

'He will be!' roared Venerio.

Arno appeared, pushing a trolley of dishes containing ravioli and charred vegetables.

'Master,' said Arno in oily, submissive tones, 'my wife has made this speciality *primo*. If you approve, it will be served at your wedding banquet.' he continued attentively. His weathered face creasing in a sly smile, he cast a fleeting glance in my direction, his eyes glinting like a fox stalking his prey.

As the old man served generous portions to the three men, deliberately excluding Inez, I felt a wave of relief wash over me and as adrenaline pulsed through my veins. Within minutes, pain and paralysis began to restrict their movements as the lethal fungi released its tendrils of poison into their bodies. One by one, they fell to the floor clutching their throats, beads of perspiration coating their reddened faces as they rolled on the floor in agony.

'Don't let them vomit! They must not be allowed to vomit. If they survive, they will murder us all," shouted Arno, gripping Alex's jaw.

Inez grabbed a knife, severed her restraints and leapt to her feet. She proceeded to kick Venerio in the head and genitals until he lay still and lifeless. The third man, Alex's friend, had been first to finish his poisonous ravioli, and lay writhing on the floor. Arno held his jaw shut until death claimed him.

It was over now; we could breathe again… But then there was Flora, I suddenly remembered. She knew everything. *Time enough to deal with her,* I told myself.

Arno and Inez took one long hour to free me of my chains, while Arno's wife attended to my feet.

'*Signore*, you are a fortunate man, there are no serious fractures. You are strong and you will recover in time. Now, find your strength, *signore,* and quickly. We alone cannot throw these imbeciles into the canal.' Of course she was right, Arno's wife was invariably right. We would struggle, even with Inez's help,

For the remaining hours of darkness, we dragged the bodies of our enemies through the principal water gate then, with a long oar, pushed them into the canal and closed the gate, as peals rang out from the campaniles heralding a new day.

Arno, his wife, and Inez then set about rinsing away the bloodstains with salt water, while I collapsed into the nearest bed. There would be repercussions when Vanerio was identified, and the authorities would stand at the door asking pertinent questions – questions that would never be truthfully answered. If our luck held, the authorities would assume they had all fallen drunk into the canal.

Hours later, Arno woke me with my phone in his hand which, fortunately for me, he had retrieved from Vanerio's pocket prior to his death.

'The young *signora* wants to speak to you. She is asking questions I dare not answer. We must take care, *signore*, these old walls have ears, and the authorities may mistrust our account of how the imbeciles died,' he said, thrusting the phone into my hand.

'I agree with Arno, we can talk later,' Aria told me. 'When are you coming home?'

'Inez will take me to the airport tomorrow and I will text you the flight information. Will you collect me? Walking is difficult right now.' There was time enough for her to see my injuries, and no point in causing her more anxiety than necessary.

'Yes, of course. We are all desperate to hear your news. Gaston, please leave Venice immediately. I want you here with me and Luc, please hurry.' A click, and she was gone.

'Hurry,' she'd said. If only I could grow wings, I would fly away and never return. This would definitely be the last time my feet would touch Venetian soil, but before leaving there were important matters to discuss with Inez. Matters that could not wait until tomorrow. She had gone to her room after helping to sluice the bloodied parts of the grand hall and exterior pathways.

She answered my call, her voice sounding hoarse, and reluctantly admitted to having cried all night.

'We need to talk, but not here. Meet me downstairs in an hour,' I told her.

'Gaston, I had intended never to see or speak to you again, but circumstances have changed and I have Luc to consider. But don't imagine our meeting will be a conciliatory reunion; that ship sank into the abyss with Giselle. I will hear what you have to say, but don't assume anything,' she replied crisply.

An hour later, aided by two walking sticks, I met Inez in the great hall. Neither of us spoke as we set off to find a more private place to discuss the serious implications of our situation. Looking across the table in a tiny back street wine bar, I could see a woman driven to the edge of insanity by a lifetime spent avoiding the appalling crimes of both of her husbands – first, Henry Roxberg, then Guido Faconi. And now, after the untimely deaths of both daughters, she had become an emotional wasteland, devoid of faith and hope.

'You must leave and soon. The authorities here are not convinced that Giselle's death was an accident, on account of her injuries. If the *carabinieri* discover a link between her death and that of Venerio and his accomplices, we can expect a knock on the door of Palazzo Faconi very soon. Also, if the results of her post mortem examination reveal any DNA connection to Venerio, they may decide to investigate further into our family's past. Their prying will become a relentless quest for the truth, then our dark secrets will return to haunt us all.'

She became increasingly restless, anxiety creasing her brow with lines of grief as she grasped my sleeve, her reddened eyes searching nearby tables for eavesdroppers.

'Gaston, don't you remember anything of me, or of your ten years as my son-in-law? You were my reliable source of adventurous bohemianism, with a light dusting of common sense. We used to laugh, cry, and argue... oh goodness, did we argue. But I loved you as a son, and now you are lost to me, along with my beautiful daughters.'

I looked away, not knowing how to respond or comfort her, so deep was the depth of her grief. Then she looked up, her eyes flaring in anger.

'It's my fault. Everything is *my* fault,' she retorted with subdued vehemence. 'Marrying Henry Roxberg was a farce from the start – his mistress saw to that. And then after he died, his bequest of the diamonds became a symbol not only of our unconventional marriage, but of our daughters. In hindsight, I regret not giving Guido his alleged share of the diamonds. Both he and his hideous family might have allowed us to live out our lives in peace, but no, I resisted, kept them hidden, denying all knowledge of them until forced to admit to lying.' She stared fixedly into the dark waters of the canal, unable to continue lamenting.

We sat in silence for a while, contemplating our futures. I caught the waiter's eye and ordered more wine and a pastry to share. The late afternoon sun had all but disappeared under a gauze of light mist swirling in from the lagoon, but we lingered on, seeking solace in our misery. Taking her hand felt awkward and unnatural. I felt her sorrow, but nothing more tangible. She needed comfort, not a lecture on how to overcome adversity. Nevertheless, I blundered on regardless.

'Inez, this may sound heartless, but we cannot change the past. You *have* a future, so for heaven's sake don't give up. You have Luc, and children need caring grandparents. It helps them understand life's timeline.

'Presumably, you will stay on in Venice until after Giselle's cremation,' I went on. 'Arno and his wife will need your support. As you say, if the authorities discover connections between the deaths, we could all be facing lengthy prison sentences.'

I got to my feet with difficulty and checked my watch. 'Time to go. Arno will be wondering where we are.'

As we approached the palazzo's front water gate, to our horror we saw two *carabinieri* leaving.

'They didn't waste any time,' I cursed. 'Hopefully they came looking for you with news of Giselle's post mortem, and not the deaths of our recently departed enemies.'

Something told me to send Inez on alone, then suddenly Arno called to warn me that Venerio's floating corpse had been found and identified by an undercover agent working for the authorities.

'*Signore*, the *carabinieri* are suspicious. They have been here asking many questions. When they find the other bodies, they will return with more questions. *Signore*, I stripped the imbeciles' bodies of identification before throwing them into the canal, but Venerio is known in this city. You must leave Venice immediately and never return. You took no part in their deaths, and you should not be blamed for my sins. I will delete the numbers in my phone and throw it into the canal. I am an old man and my life is nearing the end. Who will listen to me?'

'Arno, go and rest,' I said. 'Leave this to me.'

Inez turned to me, her face a picture of concern. 'I cannot leave yet, my absence will be regarded as callous and uncaring by the coroner,' she said. 'We must behave naturally so as not to raise suspicion. By the time they discover Alex was an employee of mine, I will be with my cousins in Madrid. And you, Gaston, is there nothing I can do to help you?'

'Yes, Inez, there is. Stay silent, keep my secret, and in return you will be allowed full access to Luc.' I kissed her cheek then limped away into the mist.

'Hey, Gaston, you came back to see me? What have you done to your foot?' It was the waitress who provided me with the sanctuary of her home on my previous visit.

'What are you doing here?' she asked. 'Let me buy you a drink.'

Our chance meeting might provide me with a bed for the night, if my luck was in.

'I'm here on business,' I lied. 'Had an accident and twisted my ankles. Would you lend me your couch for the night, no strings attached? My flight leaves at lunchtime tomorrow. I'll pay you, of course.'

She hesitated while studying me intently, deciding whether or not to grant my request.

'So, nothing's changed. You Frenchmen are still full of crap, and yes you can stay. But my bed is so much softer than my couch.'

Damn this woman's libido! Gathering my patience, and to avoid being seen in public places, such as hotels, I agreed.

'Never refuse a lady,' I replied brightly.

She smiled and took my arm, satisfied that on this occasion she had backed a winner. There was time enough later to invent a reason to avoid sexual intimacy.

As we meandered to her house, my laborious progress became more difficult with every painful step.

'I'll cook for us. What do you like to eat, seafood? Yes, we'll have oysters.' She winked seductively, but her decisive manner and obvious enthusiasm for my company had robbed me of my appetite. Having spent many years devising ways to persuade women to disrobe, it would be of no use when faced with one that could not wait to get naked.

'Let's take it slow and eat out,' I suggested.

'More French crap.' she murmured quietly, turning away to hide her embarrassment. '*Signore*, I feel you are not inclined to indulge me. Your body language and facial expressions are not that of a satisfying lover.' Understandably, she was upset at my taking advantage of her lust for me, while offering nothing in return.

'My mistake, *signore*. Enjoy your lonely couch, and please be sure to close the door firmly when you leave.'

She went to her bedroom, slamming the door behind her. Hours later, she appeared looking fabulously sexy and ready to party. However, I had no regrets as she ignored me and sailed out, slamming the front door with such force it shook the house to its foundations.

Next morning, I woke early and grabbed my phone to ring Aria. Seeing a missed call from Flora sent my temper into overdrive. The prospect of a serious face-to-face conversation with her since discovering her treachery would be something to saviour, but not now, and not here in a strange house where walls may have ears.

'Gaston, where is Alex? What have you done? There have been news reports coming out of Venice saying three bodies have been found floating in the canals. If you have harmed him, I will inform the authorities of your involvement in Guido Faconi's death.'

'Hey, slow down. I took a severe beating, due to your two-faced infamy. You betrayed me to Alex, and if that's your warped idea of love and affection, I will save Jules from an unhappy marriage.'

She broke into sobs, but I knew she would hear the news soon enough.

'Flora, Alex is dead as a result of his deception. Did you know he was Henry Roxberg's son? He and Vanerio were accomplices. Their intention to steal the Roxberg diamonds, and anything they could get their greedy hands on, has backfired. So tell me, why are you grieving for someone you hardly knew?'

'Hardly knew,' she snorted with derision. 'You know nothing. He became my lover after our first meeting. I am carrying his child, and he said we would be together when he gained control of Inez's fortune. Now he is dead, my life is ruined.'

'No chance Jules could be the father?'

'Gaston, I am two months gone; Jules and I have been together for just three weeks. Yes, he is a great guy, but unlikely to accept another man's child. If you hadn't met Aria, we could have married then raised our children together. Are you really going to marry her?'

'Yes, Flora, I really am going to do just that, and as soon as possible. Now let me give you some friendly advice. Marry Jules and make a life for yourself. He has offered to buy my property at Menton, enabling Aria, Luc, and me to make a permanent move to Antibes. Look, we both need our loved ones right now, so get real and get married.' I went on, 'Flora, listen to me. Hide your secrets, as I will hide mine. It's time now to disassociate ourselves with our past by planning for the future, and now I really must leave this city. Goodbye.'

There was no sign of my irate host. Her bed covers had not been disturbed and her extensive collection of sex toys lay unused on the shelf above her headboard. No doubt she had lingered with one of her more accommodating lovers overnight.

My throbbing toes had changed colour from deep purple to a livid pink, and a growing feeling of apprehension began to envelop me as I limped to the shower.

Aria rang to say the murders had been reported in the press, with extensive media coverage on every live stream. She said the carabinieri's suspicions had been raised by the absence of any formal identification on the bodies. If they attributed alcohol or drugs as the cause of death, they had correctly assumed some form of identification would have been found.

Eventually they would find connections – first to Inez, then to her extended family, including me. I had borne witness to three murders, each one a necessity to protect my family. What did I care if they were dead? They were thieving dirt, and they deserved to die.

Stepping out into the cool morning air, I encountered two women in close conversation. While hurrying past, they glanced in my direction with expressions of mild disgust. No doubt they thought of me as just another customer, one of many satisfied men to leave this house of amusement and pleasure. I felt exposed and vulnerable, wary of street cameras whose intrusive scrutiny sought to probe the secret world of people like me; people with something to hide.

At the airport, the eyes of my fellow passengers scanned their phone screens for images of the deceased, listening avidly to the extended news coverage of the tragic accidents to befall the three men drowned in the labyrinthine network of Venetian canals. When their post mortem results were revealed, I would be at home in France with Aria and Luc, rebuilding my business, my life, and my sense of humour.

The past year had descended into a horrific pantomime drama, and now, with the final curtain now in sight, we would leave Arno and Inez to face a potential full-scale investigation if foul play was suspected. Hopefully, the authorities would conclude the men were drunk and had fallen, much like Venerio's cousin Guido, who fell into the harbour at Villefranche-sur-Mer. All memories of that day still eluded me, and I wondered when this nightmare would end.

Lost in thought, I turned to check the departure screen, when suddenly a tap on my shoulder sent tendrils of panic up my spine.

'Your passport, *signore.*' The carabinieri thrust a hand in my direction. 'please state your business here in Venice.'

'A short holiday visit to your beautiful city.' Sweat began to form on my brow.

'Your address, please, *signore.*' I stared at him, my mind a complete blank, then I remembered the girl from the café and her address written in my pocket notebook.

As he read the address, his face fell into a picture of distaste. 'Are there no pleasure houses left in France, *signore?*'

'I was unaware at the time of booking, that anything other than bed and breakfast would be offered,' I told him.

He gave me a look of self-righteous scorn, handed back my passport, turned on his heel, and walked away.

I immediately rang Aria to recount the incident, which had left me feeling both shaken and profoundly relieved.

'I will be waiting when you arrive at Nice. But Gaston, there has been a change of plan. Jules insists we join him at his villa. He sounded upset but wouldn't say why. He said he and Flora would explain later. Apparently, they are expecting a guest and need you to be present when he or she arrives.' She paused. 'Gaston, are you still there?'

'Yes, we are about to board. See you soon.'

My mind reeled with a host of questions. Obviously, Flora had told Jules about her pregnancy, but had she told him the child was not his? Knowing Jules, he would have prised the truth out of her. So, why did Aria and I have to be involved? Hadn't we been through enough misery these past months? And who was their mystery guest?

As the plane took off, I settled down with a double espresso and a bar of chocolate, to indulge in a period of serious speculation. Jules and Mama had filled my memory gaps with their patchy recollections of my life prior to Vanerio's first attempt on my life, but there had to be so much more. It would be cruel to expect Inez to recount all of my ten-year marriage to Giselle – and ultimately, did I really want to re-live those lost years? So, back to the facts.

Alex was Henry Roxberg's son. How well these people kept their secrets and planned their carefully timed entrance into our lives. His slow-burning relationship with Inez had just been a front for stealing her diamonds, and she had fallen for it. We all fell for his bohemian attitude to life, but now that conniving bum had no life.

I presumed the Faconi/Roxberg connection had been instigated by Henry. Jules said they had stolen or replicated art, antiques, and anything else they could get their hands on from their headquarters at Roxberg Gate – that crumbling edifice to crime in the north of England, unlike Jules's villa where the welcome was always warm and the champagne ice cold.

Chapter Thirteen

She looked stunning, standing there in her favourite white linen dress, holding my son in her arms, shielding his eyes from the sun. Her face lit with relief when she caught sight of me. Running towards them, my heart soared with love and gratitude for my beautiful, steadfast Aria. As we kissed, Luc pounded both our faces with his outstretched plump palms. He was growing in confidence, like all children who know they are loved.

'Your parents are anxious for news, but we can ring them from the car. Gaston, is this where it ends? Are we safe? Can we breathe again?'

'*Ma chérie*, I cannot tell you what I do not know. Together we'll strive to put the past behind us, but there are those who know our darkest secrets. So, we must be vigilant, keep their friendship, monitor their changes in mood or circumstances, and hold our breath at cocktail parties lest they inadvertently disclose more than we would wish. There are times when our closest friends can be our worst enemies.'

'You mean Flora.'

I nodded. 'Flora is a constant threat. I suspect she has told Jules about her pregnancy, and he has taken it badly. You see, the child is not his.'

Aria came to an abrupt halt.

'My God! Don't tell me it's your child, is it, Gaston? Is Flora's child yours.'

'No, *cherie*, that dubious pleasure belongs to a dead man. Alex Forbes, to be precise, so I think we are in for more turmoil and accusations at Jules's villa.'

'I would rather have stayed with your mama and papa. It's not good for Luc to hear adults quarrelling.'

'What, and miss all the action?' She pulled a face. 'I think you've had enough action to last your lifetime.'

A soft sea breeze rippled Aria's hair as I kissed her tenderly; a kiss that was both an ending and a beginning.

'We are going to make lots of children,' I whispered into her perfumed hair.

'I think we have made a start; no red flag this month,' she replied with a confident smile.

A surge of joy coursed through my body. I would spend the rest of my life loving my Madonna from Morocco; my keeper. Every day I would draw nourishment from her well of strength. We walked, hands clasped, along the beach, every step urging us forward into our new life.

'Gaston, we must leave. Jules is expecting us.'

'Ok,' I agreed. 'Let's get it over. Tomorrow we leave for Antibes. Shall we marry on a beach in Morocco?'

'No, no, we will marry in Rome. My cousin is a priest, and he will perform the ceremony. Now we really must leave,' she urged. 'Do you need a change of clothes? We can call into your café. Is there nothing you wish to take as a memento?'

I shook my head. 'You forget I have no memory of that place, so why would I cherish something that is meaningless?'

Aria raised her eyebrows at my offhand reply. The sky had darkened, and cool breezes laden with droplets of seawater filled the air.

'Time to go. No regrets.' We kissed, then drove away and never looked back.

* * *

When we arrived at his villa, Jules came out to greet us. He appeared affable, and asked if we would like to walk around the garden before nightfall.

'Please excuse me, Jules, I need to attend to Luc. Perhaps tomorrow before we leave,' said Aria, disappearing into the villa carrying my son, who had had enough of captivity and was demanding his dinner.

'Right, Jules, what's going on?' I asked.

Just then, a taxi containing one passenger entered the drive. The passenger paid the driver, then leapt out and walked towards us.

'Might know ye would be here. Trouble follows ye around. Ye look terrible. Serves ye right.' She sounded vicious and in no mood for repartee.

'Iona, what an unpleasant surprise. I might say the same to you.'

'I'm family. Now, where is Flora?' she said flatly.

'Iona, you must be tired after your journey,' said Jules, smiling broadly. Little did he realise his reserves of charm were about to receive a battering.

'I think Flora is in the kitchen, helping to prepare dinner,' Jules said. 'She has a room ready for you.'

'Fetch her!' she snapped. 'I'm not staying here with the likes of him.' She pointed in my direction.

'Remember, you came to us. And I'm staying, so state your business then leave if you wish. Your choice,' I replied hotly, then headed indoors to find the drinks cabinet.

Minutes later, Flora appeared looking tearful and apprehensive. As she rushed over, Iona put a hand out to stop her.

'Sit down, all of you,' she commanded, as Jules handed her a large cognac and a plate of savoury biscuits.

Iona drank the cognac then sank into the nearest chair, her head lowered, composing herself for the revelations to come. Then she looked up at Flora, her eyes glistening with tears.

'Flora, ye are no orphan, ye are mine. My daughter. Henry Roxberg was yer father. I should have told ye, but the shame would have killed me. And now you've gotten pregnant by Alex, your own half-brother, so it's incest. The bairn will be damaged; ye'll have to get rid of it,' Iona shouted.

She looked frantically around the room for allies. 'How was I to know they would ever meet, let alone fall victim to fornication? And before you ask, Henry looked after me. He was kind and I loved him. He gave us a respectable home, a living, and a good life. Inez just turned her head and lived her own life,' she said defensively.

'Iona, I will not abort my baby – not for you, or for anyone. In my heart, you have always been my mother, but don't ask me to murder Alex's child.'

'Flora, it's not murder. The child is tainted, ye canna keep a tainted bairn,' implored Iona.

'Enough,' said Flora, clamping her hands over her ears. 'Jules has offered to stand by me, although hearing this he may change his mind. If so, I will raise the child alone, as you did.'

I hardly dared breathe. Alex had thrown the dice and lost his life, but then he and Venerio had been the aggressors. In life, there were winners and losers, and currently I was winning and would make sure it stayed that way.

'Dinner is served,' called Aria from the hallway.

No-one moved, except for me. Like Luc, my hunger could not wait. On the dining room table sat an assortment of pastas, sauces, and salads, and several bottles of wine. Aria and I had not eaten a decent meal in days, so we ate and waited for the others to drift in.

Eventually, the tense atmosphere dissipated as the evening wore on. Iona drank rather freely and decided to stay after all. We all sat around the table openly discussing our plans for the future.

'Aria and I intend to settle in Antibes. Papa's old bookshop will become my office. And you, Jules, have you any new projects in mind?'

'Glad to hear you're staying close,' he replied. 'Yes, Project Flora. After our wedding, Flora will run Café Fleur, formerly Villande, in Menton, and your old apartments upstairs will be transformed into holiday accommodation.'

'On the subject of weddings,' interjected Aria, 'if you and Flora agree, perhaps we can celebrate together with a double wedding? We are all of the same faith, so let's have one big party.'

'And what about me? Where will I live?' piped up Iona. 'Don't think I'm leaving my daughter to manage the poor bairn and a business. I'll have your old flat in the basement under the café,' she stated firmly.

'Good luck with that one, Jules. Fortunately, this villa is at a safe distance,' I joked. No-one laughed; no-one dared.

'Seriously, Gaston, there is something you should know. Guido Faconi was a strong swimmer with a weak heart. Yes, you pushed him into the sea, but according to the coroner's report it was a heart attack that killed him. Alex deceived you. He deceived us all,' sighed Flora.

'So, I am off the hook. No more looking over my shoulder or avoiding gendarmes. Is there any champagne in the house?' No-one was fooled by my casual humour, least of all me. But we toasted my great escape from criminality, then carried our coffee and cognacs out into the terrace.

A feeling of sublime peace washed over me as we sat enjoying the evening twilight. Birds sang, fireflies danced, and even Iona's foul mood mellowed under the influence of alcohol and sincere good humour. We talked and drank till midnight, then Jules remembered something.

'Flora, darling, where is the parcel that arrived this morning for Gaston?'

'Oh, I forgot. It's on the desk in your study.'

'How strange. Why would anyone write to me here?' I said.

Aria shrugged. 'Well, open it and find out.'

I carefully removed the many layers of wrapping, and a dawning realisation came to me as a glimpse of red velvet appeared. Further unwrapping revealed a drawstring bag in the shape of a heart, the contents of which were hard and unyielding to my touch. Suddenly I had a searing flashback.

'Aria, I know what is in this bag.' I placed a silver salver on the table, then emptied the laser show that was the Roxberg diamonds onto the tray. Moments of stunned silence passed as the dazzling jewels threw spears of piercing light around the room.

A note from Inez read:

My dear Gaston,

The Roxberg legacy will live on with you, and with whom you choose to share my tainted diamonds. Choose wisely.

Sincerely,
Inez

Epilogue

The castellated ruins of Roxberg Gate lie undisturbed by ghosts of the past. Now seabirds nest and ferns seed, as lichens invade this mansion of tragedy and death.

Fox cubs romp where children played; mice colonise while woodworms feast.

After nightfall, when owls hoot and spirits haunt, we humans envelope our strengths and frailties in veils of slumber.

At dawn, we rise to unleash our multifaceted characters into our ever-changing world – a secret world where avarice and greed are celebrated, where infidelity, dishonour, and cruelty thrive in the cesspool of modern society.

Throughout this enthralling trilogy, my characters have displayed one or all of these traits. Nevertheless, I have enjoyed beyond measure bringing them all to life.

Acknowledgements

My grateful thanks to the whole team at Grosvenor House Publishing for their professional support and thoughtful guidance. Also to friends Sarah Cotton, Susan Main and Mary Reardon.

My home is situated in the medieval quarter at
Stratford upon Avon; nestling peacefully in a
quintessentially English garden behind the Guildhall,
where William Shakespeare began his studies.

The Bards potent influence surrounds my
daily life. I walk where he walked,
see what he saw, hear what he heard and live
where he learned.